ONLY FOR US

ONLY COLORADO BOOK #6

JD CHAMBERS

Copyright © 2019 by JD Chambers

All rights reserved.

No part of this book may be reproduced in any form or by any electronic or mechanical means, including information storage and retrieval systems, without written permission from the author, except for the use of brief quotations in a book review.

Beta Reading: Leslie Copeland

Proofreading/Editing: Courtney Bassett

Cover Art: Garret Leigh, Black Jazz Design

❦ Created with Vellum

DEDICATION

*A toppy twink for the Queen of Kink
(aka Courtney Bassett)*

PROLOGUE

FIVE YEARS AGO - BOONE

"Don't be such a pussy," Dad sneers as he pushes back from the kitchen table, causing it to shake on wobbly legs. I mix my fruit, yogurt, and granola together as two sunny-side up eggs stare at me behind watery yolks. "They'll never consider you for the draft next year if you can't play through the pain."

I can practically hear what my boyfriend Arthur would say to my father's choice of words. Words I've heard directed at others all my life. His lecture clearly sounds in my head, in his voice, snooty inflection and disgusted tone and all. Something about the shared roots of misogyny and homophobia, most of which I don't really understand except that I shouldn't use the word pussy anymore.

Since the last thing I need is for my father's harping to shift from my inability to play with torn tendons and a dislocated knee to my becoming soft and sensitive while at school, I will not be sharing Arthur's thoughts on his language choices with him. I focus on the doctor's words instead.

"The doctor said I had to keep off it," I remind him, but it doesn't improve his sneer.

"When I played ball in college," he says as he hovers behind me, like his past looms over my future, beginning yet another lecture I've heard enough times to have memorized.

Torn rotator cuff.

"I had a torn rotator cuff, but it was championships, and I played through it."

The doctors had no idea.

"The doctors said they had no idea how I managed to keep pitching under that much pain."

We won.

"But I wouldn't give up, and we won. College World Series Champions 1986. Because I wasn't a pussy."

I bite back the argument that football isn't like baseball, and he didn't have the threat of a three-hundred-pound man tackling him and his shoulder, or in my case shredded knee, to the ground at least a dozen times or more a game.

Not. The. Same. Thing.

"I could kill your mother for convincing you to go on that ski trip. You should have stayed home and trained. No team cares if you're a fucking saint or not. Just look at what happened to Tebow. They care if you can play and if you're going to pussy out the second you get injured."

No convincing had been needed. I just wanted to ski, and Arapaho Basin starts earlier than most other ski areas. Getting a jump on the one activity I have left that still clears my head and I don't have to hide – priceless. I only pretended that I bought the whole "volunteering with the church youth group will be great for your career" angle so that my dad would have a reason to give in. Otherwise, I would have spent my entire fall break at the gym or running drills. Now, I won't be doing either for a while.

"Doc said he'd have a better idea if surgery is needed in a few weeks, after the swelling goes down. I'm keeping up my diet and I can work out my upper body in the meantime. I won't lose much. If I keep off it, maybe I won't have to have surgery, and I can get back on the field faster."

Dad grumbles something as he leaves the room, his striped golf shirt holding in his rapidly expanding middle-aged gut slipping from its neat tuck and exposing a bit of spare tire. I'm at twelve percent body fat, but you'd think our bodies were reversed based on how he harps on my eating and exercising habits. I've been out of commission for two weeks, and yet I haven't slid or slipped. I'm a finely tuned machine, whether he wants to admit it or not, and I'm doing everything right to get back out there as soon as I can. I trust the team's doctors and physical therapists more than I do a man whose daily exercise routine consists entirely of the increased heartrate he gets by yelling at me.

My phone picks that unfortunate moment to ding. Dad yells from the hall, "No going out with friends. If you can't play ball, you can't play at anything else."

Arthur: There's a Parks and Recreation marathon on tonight. Would you like to come over for dinner?

Boone: Can't. My dad is on my case again.

Arthur: I'm sorry. I'll miss you.

The feeling is mutual but love and understanding simply aren't what I need right now. Neither is my dad's suffocating presence. I don't know what I need, except air.

"I'm not going out with friends," I shout back down the hall at him. "I'm going to the library. There's a group paper due on Monday."

Dad makes his displeasure known as I clomp my crutches past him, grabbing at my backpack for show, but at least he doesn't try to stop me. The bus stop is at the end of our street, and thank God it isn't snowing. The weather still hasn't decided if it's fall or winter, so I'm safe with my crutches. I have a feeling I'd go down like Roberto Duran if there was ice on the ground.

Fifteen minutes and a bus that smells like Fritos later, I make my way to the counter at FoCo Coffee Haus and place my order. I don't know why my dad can't settle down and be content with his own life. Why he feels he has to push me, whether it's something I want or not. It's a miracle I still love football, considering it's one more thing I have to keep up in order to prove to my father that I'm a man. Arthur read an article to me on toxic masculinity once. I'm not sure if he was trying to be subtle or not, but no matter how much the article made sense, that logic can't overpower the voice in my head telling me I have to please my dad and make him proud of me.

That voice overrides everything.

"Skinny caramel macchiato."

I grab my coffee, ignoring the mental voice that sounds suspiciously like my father, berating me for my choice in beverage. "That is not what an athlete drinks. Do you want to get fat? If your performance drops ..."

I have too many voices in my head.

"You're sitting in my seat."

Great, now there's one more.

A gorgeous blond whose graceful movements could have been choreographed stands before me, slapping down a handful of napkins and jarring the table. My latte sloshes over the side of my cup, the foam jiggling in place, but the creamy liquid underneath seeping through the sides and over the edge.

"This isn't kindergarten. We don't have assigned seats." I grab one of his napkins and dab at the side of my cup. This is the best seat in the whole of FoCo Coffee Haus – near the window that overlooks the Oval and some of the prettier older buildings on campus. It is also far enough in the corner that you can remain invisible while nursing your coffee and your feelings. I'm not about to give it up to some twinky brat, no matter how pretty.

Only for Us

"You're right, but most people still consider it rude to sit on someone else's coat."

I look behind me and sure enough, I'm squashing a quilted red coat draped over the back. Next to my cup on the table sits a plate with a half-finished bagel and a to-go cup of coffee. Not sure how I missed it. My argument with my dad must have rattled me more than I thought.

"Here." He leans over me and tugs at his coat. The scent of warm spices, like curling in front of a fire with a mug of cider, wafts over me as he invades my space. The smooth, creamy skin of his neck is so close, I could tilt my head an inch and nuzzle it with my nose. I can't drag my eyes away from that skin, even as I shift and allow him to pull his coat out from behind me.

"Since you're injured," he says, "I will be the bigger man and move seats. But I'm only letting it slide this once. Next time, I'll have to punish you."

He finishes his statement with a wink, and my swallow lodges in my throat. His eyelids thin to narrow slits as he takes in my bobbing Adam's apple and heaving chest and wide eyes.

"Oh, honey," he whispers. "I'll punish you anyway, if that's what you want."

My answer must be written across my face, because he grabs my coffee cup and straightens from his position leaning over me. "I'm going to get this to go. My apartment is right around the corner."

I've never been spoken to like this before, and it lights up my insides like I'm a jack-o-lantern and it's Halloween.

There have been times when I look at Arthur and I can see him holding back. But I have no idea how to tell him what I want, or that I think we might want the same things. Hell, just telling him that I wanted to bottom was hard enough.

I'm not out at school; I have no interest in making headlines for my orientation and not my skill. But when I met Arthur, it was impossible to deny when he led me away from the party and to his house to make love to me for the first time. I'd only ever had anonymous hookups before that, and the way Arthur cared for me was addictive.

I do care for Arthur too, but it doesn't feel like enough anymore. Even after all our time together, he has never ordered me around or threatened me with punishments. Arthur's a big guy, quite a bit taller than me, actually. He could get away with it, where most people would be too scared of my size. But every time I think my eyes must be pleading for it, he backs away.

Yet here is this guy, half my size, bossing me around without any hesitation.

"Let's go." He hands over my coffee and shrugs into his coat, tugging where his hair gets caught under the collar on one side. The other side is shaved and my hands twitch to feel the soft prickles against my skin.

With his coat on, he takes my coffee back – now holding a cup in each hand – and steps back to allow me to grab my crutches and pull myself up. When I'm ready, he turns and exits the coffee shop without a second glance to ensure I'm following. I get the impression he'd stomp off with my coffee in hand either way.

As we turn the corner and approach his apartment building from the outside, I recognize the place. One of Arthur's friends lives here, a guy that doesn't like me much. Just because I'm good at sports doesn't mean I'm an idiot, even if his closeted jock statements weren't so thinly veiled. We enter the courtyard and approach door 104. If I remember correctly, Arthur's friend is just a couple doors down, but that isn't my only concern. This whole complex is teeming with CSU students. What if someone sees me?

"You don't have to worry. I live alone," he says, ushering me through the door and down the hallway. No lingering or pretense. "No one's going to see you with me, and anyone who might recognize you is probably glued to the TV right now or at the game already."

Damn, do my eyes tell my whole story to every other gay man out there? Or just this one?

"I might find the game boring, but those tight pants most certainly are not. I know who you are. Now strip and get on the bed, face up."

He pulls a pillow from under the covers of the bed that takes up most of the room in his small bedroom, fluffs it a few times and tosses it at the head of the bed. I don't think my fingers have ever moved so fast as I strip off my shirt and coat. My knee brace has too many damn straps, and soon cool hands still mine.

"Do you need to keep the brace on?"

"No, I just can't put any weight on the knee."

"Well, there goes my ideas for spanking."

My feelings on the subject must be clear as day across my face, because he takes one look at me and laughs. "Another time, when your knee is better, I will owe you a spanking, sweetheart."

He helps me undo my brace and remove my sweatpants without putting my legs back down for support. I push against my good leg until I'm in position and lie down against the pillow he set out for me. My cock bounces and smacks my stomach with every scooch until I relax in place and then it stands proudly, waiting for the punishment I've been promised.

"Put your hands behind the pillow and keep them there. If you have to grip the pillow to keep them in place, you may. But that's my favorite pillow, and I'm going to be pissed if you mess it up."

I doubt there will be much pillow left if he keeps talking to me like that.

He pulls off his long-sleeved shirt and slowly peels his tight jeans from his lean legs. No underwear. My fingertips itch with want, but I tighten my fists around his pillow instead.

His hands roam over his own body, pinching at his nipples, swirling around the bare skin just above his long cock. He carefully straddles me, and my cock jumps as if it has a mind of its own and wants to touch the beautiful penis just a breath away. His hand closes around himself, and I can feel the air around us move as he strokes himself, using his precum as lube. My own precum drips from my tip, leaving a pool below my belly button.

"You were a thoughtless boy, weren't you? Taking my table." His voice surprises me and I realize I have been fixated on his cock. His eyes sparkle when I check his face to see if I've been caught.

Of course I have.

He continues to jerk himself, every thrust an imaginary one to me. His thighs graze mine, but otherwise he holds himself back enough to avoid touching me in any way. His other hand still caresses his chest, his stomach, his neck.

"A thoughtless boy who thought I would happily give in because you're the school's golden boy. Or maybe because you're injured. But it never crossed your mind that you were wrong, did it? That you were being rude and thoughtless."

His hand moves faster now, more precum slicking his way, and my cock throbs in time with his hand. Every pump of his fist ghosts across my dick too. His finger dips into his mouth, his tongue darting out to lick the pad and then suck it further in against his hollowed cheeks. His eyes close and his head tilts back as streams of cum shoot from his dick, splattering my thighs and balls and earning an extra thump of my dick as a strand lands across it. God, it's so hot, I'm about ready to blow, just from the visuals. He hasn't touched me. Not once.

"You think it's your turn?" he says with a wicked gleam, and the muscles in my thighs and buttocks almost spasm with relief.

Blond hair tickles my left cheek as he leans forward, keeping his body out of the sticky mess, and licks against the seam of my lips.

"No, you didn't think I was going to let you come, did you?" He leans back, his ass against his heels, and laughs. "This is your punishment for not thinking of others." I never knew punishments could be so creative and effective. Just the thought of his denial makes me harder than I've ever been before. "Come back here tomorrow, same time, same place. If you've touched yourself, I'll know. But if you've been good and taken your punishment, I'll make you fly."

I wonder if it will feel like it does when I fly down the side of the mountain on my skis. Or the way it used to feel like my heart would fly out of my chest when one of my passes landed squarely in the hands of a teammate for a winning touchdown. I'd give anything to fly again.

Before I realize what's happening, he is gently lifting my injured leg to slide my boxers back up my body. He's not even going to let me clean up? Fuck, that shouldn't be so hot. The gleam in his eye says he knows it.

Once I have my clothes back on, his hand pats my cheek and he helps me to my crutches. I should be grossed out right now, sticky with someone else's cum, but I feel good. Wanted. My head is so far in the clouds, I'm not sure if I'll ever come down, or if I even want to.

He opens his front door to show me out, and suddenly everything comes crashing down. Or crashing sideways. Or just plain crashing as I stumble into a broad chest and someone grabs then quickly releases me.

Arthur.

Punishment for not thinking of others. That's what he said. He had no idea just how right he was.

1
JAY

"I changed my mind. I'm not coming." I clutch my phone in my hand, trying my best not to turn back and look into the mirror.

"You have to come," Kieran says. "I never throw parties for exactly this reason."

"Liar, you always throw parties. You are one big excuse to throw a party."

"Fine, but only because my friends have promised to come. And you promised."

"But my hair looks like something a sick dog hacked up."

"It can't be that bad. You're just a drama queen. This is our first party as a living-together couple. You have to be there."

My best friend Kieran and his boyfriend Ted have been together for almost a year now, but they took their time before moving in together. Part of the reason was not wanting to alienate their respective roommates – Kieran's friend Ben, who everyone agrees would lose his head if it wasn't attached, and Ted's nephew Jonathan, who as a grad school student benefitted from living rent-free with his relative. All good reasons to keep to the status quo, but partly it was also not wanting to rush things.

It took a long time for Kieran and Ted to get together, and I think they were both just happy to have made it that far.

The problem is, Kieran and Ted come pre-packaged with a large group of friends. All of whom will be at this party. And all of whom will have some preconceived notion about me. I've come to accept that and move on. I'm not in control of what they think of me, but I am in control of how they see my hair, and I am not showing my face with this fried, grey-streaked rat's nest.

I cover my face as I snap a selfie and shoot it to Kieran. I can hear the ding when he receives it, and then the "oh."

"Can't Stephanie fix it?"

"She's on vacation," I say as I decide to move as far away from the mirror as possible and flop onto my bed. "That's how this happened in the first place."

I would usually never trust my hair to anyone but Stephanie, but like I said, everyone is going to be at this party. I wanted to impress.

A dry, crackly strand of grey flops over my forehead and into my eyes.

I'm going to make an impression alright.

"You could just pull it back into a ponytail like you do at work."

"Can you make it a costume party? Then I could cover it up with a hat or something."

Kieran's laughter is evident, even if he manages to keep it from being audible over the phone.

"I'm not turning it into a costume party; it's in less than two hours. Which reminds me, I need to get going. I sent Ted on a final liquor store run, but I've been cleaning all day and I need a shower."

"You had better get people so smashed, they don't remember my awful hair."

"I promise no one will be paying any attention to your hair,"

Kieran says. "If they remember anything negative, it will be Ted's vegan meatless-balls. I love most of his creations, but those fuckers are just weird. And so ripe for Ben jokes."

He snorts into the phone at his own double entendre. I swear, between Ben and Jonathan, my sweet, innocent best friend is getting corrupted. Granted, with the way his red cheeks highlight his freckles until his entire head seems to glow as bright as his reddish-orange hair, I can't deny them that fun. An embarrassed Kieran is adorable.

"Get here early, and I'll let you borrow my beanie."

"What color is it?"

Silence.

"What? I have to make sure I match."

"Oh. My. God. Goodbye, Jay."

By the time I leave for the party, my bedroom looks like a tornado came through, which is par for the course on a night out for me. I've tried on more outfits than normal since I didn't bother to do anything with my hair other than pull it back into a bun, and finally settled on skinny white ripped jeans and a black tank top with a rainbow foil design. Black and white and rainbow. That will surely match any beanie that Kieran has, even if the beanie will look totally out of place.

Never, ever again will I make a rash decision about my hair.

I usually bike everywhere, but since their housewarming presents are breakable, I get an Uber. I arrive ten minutes early, with a bottle of wine in one hand and in the other, a rustic box of jars filled with dirt that makes Ted's eyes light up.

"Is that ...?"

"A makeshift herb garden. I started it a couple of weeks ago, so hopefully you'll begin to see some action soon."

Ted takes it from my hands and sets it down on the dining table, which is decorated and probably the last place Kieran wants anything that could get things dirty, but before I'm able to point this out to Ted, I'm engulfed in warm arms and an earthy, sweet scent.

"Thank you, Jay. That was really thoughtful."

I have no idea why his hug makes me choke up. It isn't like I've never been hugged before. But something about its sincerity has me suddenly realizing that I'm missing this in my life, and I'm aching for it.

"I better go find Kieran," I say, extracting myself before I give in and decide to stay there all night. Not because I have a thing for Ted – I don't – but because the crush of appreciation was addictive, and something I won't be experiencing again any time soon. Might as well get used to it.

I knock on the bedroom door at the same time as I open it, because seriously, if Kieran isn't dressed and ready by now then he deserves to be embarrassed. I find him inside their walk-in closet, one that I'm a tad jealous of. He's got his green jeans on with his red Converse, and he's sifting through shirts until he pulls out a red and green plaid button-down.

"No."

He jumps because he didn't hear me come in, even though I didn't attempt to be quiet, and then glares.

"It's my favorite," he says, holding it in front of his bare chest.

"And with those jeans and shoes, it will make you look like a Christmas elf. In April."

Kieran rolls his eyes but returns the shirt to the rack. "Then what do you recommend, oh sage fashionista?"

"Personally, I think a black mesh tee would be perfect, but since Ted probably wouldn't appreciate that–"

"At least not in public," Kieran interjects.

"Then I would recommend this," I say, and hold out a black V-neck made of soft, almost satiny material that looks incredibly yummy on Kieran. He puts it on, and I tuck in the front while he holds out his arms to allow my fussing. Some guys would look hot with their chest hair peeking from the dip in the shirt. Kieran looks hot with his freckles peeking out. Plus, the black contrasts with his pale skin, and the way it clings around his nipples is sexy and suggestive without being vulgar.

"Perfect."

He reaches up above the rack of clothes, almost undoing my excellent tucking, and brings down a grey knit beanie, the slouchy kind, which means it will cover my entire head and only a bit at my hairline will show.

"Bless you," I say, snatching it from his hands and taking it to the bathroom to primp until it sits perfectly.

"Help yourself," Kieran says with a laugh, but I know he doesn't mean it. Kieran loves me. I can see another snarky comment forming on his lips, but it's interrupted by the doorbell.

"Better get going, you hostess with the mostess."

"I don't know why I put up with you," Kieran says as he exits his room, leaving the door open because unlike me, his room is perfectly clean. No one would know he was debating outfits mere seconds ago.

"Because I'm adorable," I call after him, only to find myself facing Cameron's smirk.

"Ted told me I could throw my jacket on the bed."

There are people you know in life who are attractive or handsome or hot, and you accept that and move on. For example, I think Kieran is absolutely beautiful. And Ted, in his leather gear – which he doesn't know I've seen him in – is smoking. But then there are those people who are so far out of the league of everyday beauty that they turn your brain to mush. They're the people who end up becoming supermodels or movie stars. The ones who poets would have written stories about in ancient times, because their beauty would launch a thousand ships or start a war or lure the gods into some sort of mischief. Cameron is that kind of stunning.

Which is why my initial response is to point and say, "Bed."

"Thanks," Cameron says, removing his jacket in a way that has his torso twisting and biceps visibly flexing underneath his shirt. I bet his abs are marble-worthy, but unfortunately his shirt is too loose for confirmation. His dark skin glows, looking like satin perfection that I want to run my hands over, and he stands a full head taller than me. How I'd love to see him writhing beneath me, naked and glorious. "And yes, definitely adorable."

He winks and leaves before I have a chance to recover.

The party is a veritable minefield. Happy couples everywhere, most of which I've either hit on or been with in some way. Even Kieran came into my life through an online hookup app, though we quickly realized we were best friend material and not hookup material. Everyone knows I went on a few dates with Ben before it became obvious he expected me to bottom, and I realized it wasn't going to work out, even as casual fuck buddies. And the guys all talk enough to know that I've hit on Arthur and Jonathan and Mal at various times, before being corrected. But no one else knows that I've been with Craig and Zach, because they keep the openness of their relationship a secret from their close friends, preferring to engage in extracurricular fun outside of the Fort Collins gay community, where word would easily get back to their little group. That was a happy surprise, seeing Zach splayed out on a bed at a sex club while Craig eyed men over to help themselves.

It was only by chance that we hooked up that night in a Denver sex club, something that hasn't happened since, no matter how much I wish it had. It was quite the experience. Like, life-changing, confidence-building, world-rocking. In another reality, it would have been so earth-shatteringly good for them too that they would have opened up their relationship and invited me to be their third. But they only enjoy the kink of sharing; neither of them seem to be polyamorous in the romantic aspect of their relationship.

Instead, we tiptoed around each other for months afterwards. I could fake it, and I think Craig could have too, but Zach's blushes every time I tried to initiate even the most dull, weather-related conversations were a glaring, tomato-red flag, so I kept my distance. Now, we give each other polite nods, but pretend that we aren't close because the awkwardness of my having dated Ben, and not because of anything else.

It's a strangely uncomfortable group of friends I have unwittingly surrounded myself with.

All the food and beverages have been arranged on the dining table, so the kitchen is empty when I make my escape. I've made awkward small talk with everyone here, most looking as if I should leave them alone already, like my singledom could be catching or a curse. Maybe if Kieran and Ted had invited more of the single guys from the store, or if either of them had any close single friends other than me and Cameron, it might not be so bad. But the house is awash with happy couples, and if Kieran weren't my best friend, I would have run away hours ago.

I stare out the window into the side yard that's barely visible in the spring evening light. Another few minutes and it will be pitch black. For now, only the brightest white flowers can be seen, even though I know it's a spring wonderland of flowers back there due to Ted's green thumb.

Music pulses in the background, although no one was dancing when I made my escape, but it's loud enough to mask the sound of anyone else joining me in the kitchen. Which is why, when a smooth voice sounds mere inches behind me, I jump so much in surprise I almost bang my head into the nearby cabinet.

"You don't seem like the type to hide from a party."

I let my heartrate return to normal until I'm able to slide into my sultry smile, the one I practice in the mirror for occasions like this one.

"Maybe I was trying to lure you away from the others."

Cameron is typically an easy target for flirting, at least when I'm prepared for him and not caught off guard like in the bedroom earlier. Mostly because I know he'll never take me up on what I'm selling. Flirting with him is kind of like being able to practice your dance moves with Baryshnikov. If you can strut your stuff and not end up looking like a total idiot, it's a win. And then, when you try your moves on someone of a less godlike stature, it's like putting the training wheels back on after competing in the Tour de France. Easy peasy.

How do I know that Cameron will never bite after my shiny little lure? Because he holds himself with the confidence and self-assuredness of a top. Damn, Cameron might as well be the illustration next to the dictionary definition of "dom top." So when a twinky little waif like me tells him that he wants to stick his dick into what he can only imagine are smooth, dark globes of ass perfection, I can guarantee the answer will be, "Get lost."

That's not even taking into account the fact that Cameron lost his long-term partner to a sudden heart attack last year. He moved to Fort Collins almost immediately after, and he hasn't shown any indication that he's ready to get back out there. He's reserved and somber most of the time, and we all pretend not to notice the sad and wistful glances when Ted and Kieran are being particularly couple-y. And when I get my flirt on, he smiles at me like I'm his friend's kid brother with a cute crush, but he's not going to dissuade me because at least it gives him an ego boost, when that's about all he could ask for at the moment.

"Wanna dance? I bet I could show you some moves you've never seen before." I swivel my hips and wag my eyebrows at him, hoping for a laugh, but failing.

Only for Us

"I don't doubt that for a second," Cameron says, only managing a quick grin before turning his attention to the table filled with housewarming presents. He runs a finger along the edge of one of the herb jars. "Ted said you made this for him?"

"It doesn't look like it now, but it's an herb garden. Because Ted likes to cook."

"You're so ... you."

"I'm not sure if that's a compliment or not, but there's really nobody else I can be," I say with a shrug and turn back to the window. Cameron's eyes are too good at seeing things, probably why he's a superstar lawyer. He can smell deflection. Doesn't stop me from trying. "It's just a bunch of dirt. Chances are pretty good I killed them all before they could even start to grow. Lord knows I can't keep a house plant to save my life."

Cameron turns to mimic my position, staring out into the darkness of the night. "Sometimes I think I'm everybody but me. I picked out my apartment because I knew it was the one Dylan would choose. My clothes are courtesy of my sister, or at least her opinion of what colors and styles look good on me. I don't even know what kind of coffee is my favorite."

"Skinny mocha latte," I respond, because I know my friends' coffee drinks by heart. I've made them all enough times.

"That was Dylan's drink."

"Favorite books or movies?" I ask, slowly turning to study his profile. He remains fixated on a point outside, unwilling to look me in the eye.

"I always go see whatever friends invite me to see. I don't remember the last movie I watched because I wanted to. And I rarely watch anything at home. I'm never there long enough, always running back to the office because there's too much to do at work."

"Books?"

"I think the last book I read was *Sula* for my required English lit class in college."

Cameron's eyes drop to where his hands knead at the countertop edge, rubbing the smooth edge back and forth across his palms.

I scoot my hand over until my pinky touches his. He doesn't look at me, but stares at our contrasting hands – mine as pale as a spiderweb and his as dark as the shadowed trees outside the kitchen window.

"The next time you come in to the coffee shop," I say, infusing my voice with a confidence I hope is catching, "I am not serving you a skinny mocha latte. I'm going to give you a different drink each time until you can tell me which one is your favorite."

His eyes close, but a smile spreads across his face, giving him a serene glow.

I take it as encouragement, and add, "And try going to the movies by yourself once in a while. Pick something Dylan would have never wanted to see. I do it all the time. Well, not the Dylan part obviously, but the alone part. Mostly because no one else wants to see the movies I like, but also because it's liberating."

I was doing so well. I squeeze my own eyes shut, trying to unsee the humiliating twist of Cameron's lips when my verbal diarrhea really got going. I lift my head unnaturally high and turn on my heel.

"Now, if you'll excuse me, I have a tight booty to shake."

As I exit the room with as much flair as I can manage without tripping or flailing in some unattractive manner, I pray that Ted and Kieran are willing to dance. They're the only couple who will without acting like I'm some sort of homewrecking tart. Which is a really unfair label. I've never wrecked a single home. At least not intentionally. I just like to flirt. There's nothing wrong with that. Mal flirts and everyone acts

Only for Us

like they're the most precious thing on the planet. I do it, and lock up your husbands and boyfriends, fellas!

Kieran shakes his hips in time with the music and I join him, turning his unconscious swaying into actual dancing. Ted saunters over in time with the music and takes each of our hands, twirling us around and around, one twink per arm, until we're dizzy and laughing.

Sigh.

Just once, I'd like to be part of my own couple, and not the third wheel.

2

CAMERON

"Please come for Easter. She's worried about you. You haven't been home since Dylan," Celeste, my older sister, says as I switch the phone between hands so I can shut down my computer. I hope she lets me off easy or I'm going to be late. Serves me right for answering the phone without checking caller ID.

"I know, but come on. Dad will be swamped with tax season." He's our stepdad, but we never call him that. I was brattier than Celeste about accepting him at first, but he makes Mom happy, so we love him. "And my practice is finally getting established. You all should come here this summer instead."

Honestly, when I moved to Fort Collins, a part of me was shocked that Mom didn't move out here too. I guess even her "precious baby boy" gets outranked by grandkids. Celeste's response when I suggested my new position was that payback was a bitch. I'm glad to know she's not bitter.

I know my family well enough to know that this is only part of a massive ploy to get me back to California. Step one, Celeste and a holiday. When I didn't come home for Thanksgiving or Christmas, I got the mother of all guilt-trip care packages. My favorite cookies, homemade ornaments from my niece and nephew, and plenty of photos to show me what I was missing.

Step two, if Celeste fails, will no doubt be a visit from my mother. In fact, I'm banking on it. I want her to see how happy I am in Fort Collins. I'm sure they thought a city boy like me wouldn't last in a place where every season is an opportunity to do something different outdoors. Maybe if she understands that I'm finally in a good place, both mentally and physically, she and my father will be more supportive of the move. More visits and fewer guilt trips. It's worth a shot.

"If it's as hot here as it was last summer, I might just take you up on it."

"Mountains. Fresh, cool air. Fun for the kids. Think about it," I say, sounding vaguely like a new laundry detergent commercial. To be fair, Fort Collins gets just as hot in the summer as home *unless* you're in the mountains, but I'm not going to volunteer that information. "Come visit. Let me show you that I'm okay."

After Dylan's death, I felt like I had died too. I may not have had enough time with him, but I'd found the love of my life. Most people don't even get that much, so it felt selfish to look for more. And for the first year, all of me was on board with that plan, though that is a misnomer. Plan implies conscious decision, whereas it was more of a state of being. I was simply numb.

Then, when Ted and Kieran moved in together, the numbness that I felt thawed a little, and it wasn't so much that I longed for love, but for someone to once again share things with. Watching them with their little inside jokes and tender touches when they thought no one noticed. Having someone who simply makes you feel less alone. I'm ashamed to admit to avoiding them sometimes, because it hurts. Kieran always tries to include me in dinners and get-togethers, and he's so sweet to make me feel at home here. But now that the numbness is wearing off, I ache for the half of me that's missing.

Yet at their party, I also felt something for the first time since Dylan's death. Hope. I know he flirts with everyone, but Jay's teasing and compliments hit me in a way they hadn't before. He made me feel seen and appreciated, and something other than sad for once. He made me feel like I just might be able to move on someday, because there are kind, funny, handsome men out there who have the ability to make me smile. And smiling is a really good feeling.

So yes, I'm okay.

"You know that's all we want, right, Cam? We want you to be okay. More than okay."

"Then I mean it. Come for a visit. I'm truly not avoiding you. I'm busy. Bring the whole family if you want, although you'll need to get a hotel room. I'll take you sight-seeing. You can meet my friends, and then maybe you and Mom will finally stop worrying."

Celeste snorts into the phone. "Yeah, right. She'll just find something else to worry about."

"So true," I say with a laugh, because she's right. Kieran pokes his head into the room and waves a file folder at me. "I've got to go, but I'm going to start making plans right now. You'd better come."

"All right, all right. Bye, Cammy."

I shake my head as I hit the end button on my phone, but I wouldn't trade my crazy family for anything.

"Let me guess, your mom?" Kieran asks, entering the room now that my call has ended.

"Celeste."

"I had a fifty-fifty chance," he says, and sets the folder in my inbox, where he puts all documents that will eventually need my attention. Urgent files go on my keyboard.

"Can you get everything ready for the Jones deposition tomorrow? I'm heading out a little early. I got myself a ticket for the latest Marvel movie."

Kieran's mouth drops but he recovers quickly. "You should have invited me. I'll go see anything with Jude Law. You can't go alone. That's just ..." I quirk an eyebrow at him and his accusing hands that had seconds ago been raised in objection now clasp in front of him like a model schoolboy. "Perfectly normal and not-at-all sad behavior."

"Nice save." Kieran means well, after all. I'm not going to go into detail about how sad and pathetic I felt, talking to Jay and not even being able to identify my favorite movies. I decided to take Jay's advice and see something that Dylan would have never picked. And to be honest, it's probably something I would have never thought to pick either. "It's easier than trying to agree on a movie with someone else."

"Whenever Ted and I can't agree on a movie, I find a well-placed bet does the trick," Kieran says with a smirk.

His computer, two rooms away in the front area that serves as reception, beeps. Kieran pulls his phone from his back pocket and swipes at a notification.

"Time to water the plants," he says. "Have fun at the movies. But next time, invite me."

I pack up some files to review at home and pass him as he returns with a watering can nestled inside a knitted cozy. The potted plants have all been cozied too. Jay taught himself to knit last winter and shared his overabundance of practice pieces with the office.

Most law offices I've been in, and believe me that's a lot, tend to either have a sleek, modern feel or a stuffy, old-school vibe. With Jay's touches, via Kieran, my office feels more homey and comfortable. All I'm lacking is a fireplace and a cat. Given the nature of most of the cases I handle, I kind of love that my office

Only for Us

feels like a safe space and not someplace clinical. Maybe I should get a fireplace and a cat. Maybe I've been a cat guy all along and just didn't know it. I certainly wouldn't mind coming home to something warm and cuddly.

I should do something nice to repay Kieran for bringing the only bit of comfort into my life that I have. All I brought to their housewarming party was a bottle of wine. Maybe I can talk to Jay for ideas. He's creative and thoughtful and even though I'm not going to pursue anything with him, I'll take any chance I can get to be close to the man.

By the time I get home and changed into something more comfortable than a suit and tie, it's already time to leave for the movie theater. I chose the smaller one that will be less crowded, since I don't need to broadcast to the entire planet that I'm going alone to a movie.

My fingers drum against my thigh as I stand in line for drinks and popcorn. Normally, the line moves faster than this. I sigh and glance around, noticing the man behind me in line doing the same. He's cute, the kind that makes something in my chest flutter, but it's his expression that entrances me. His sandy-blond hair sticks up where his hands ran through it and his hazel eyes roam the theater lobby, not like he's looking for someone, but like he's making sure he isn't noticed. It makes me feel even worse when he catches me staring.

"A friend told me I needed to try going to movies by myself. Apparently, it's a sign of self-assurance."

I mentally cringe at how pathetic that sounded, but my dorkiness seems to put him at ease as his expression relaxes and I receive a smile in return.

"I've been waiting ages but didn't have anyone to see it with. Comic book movies are too nerdy, I guess."

I haven't flirted like this since high school, all shy glances and tentative smiles, but it tightens my chest and makes my head feel light.

"Boone?" The shrill-sounding woman forces my line companion's expression from calm to "oh shit" in mere seconds. "Oh my God, funny seeing you here."

Boone turns slowly, a smile tugging at his lips that looks like he's had to use fish hooks to get his mouth turning in the right direction. No amount of smiling could hide the look of sheer panic in his eyes.

"What movie are you going to see?" She grabs his hand and reads his ticket without waiting for him to answer. "Oh my God! Sonia and I are going to that too. You should join us. Sonia, this is my co-worker I was telling you about. The single one?"

Sonia reaches out a hand, but not to shake. Instead, she runs her palm from his shoulder to his biceps, squeezing along the way. Boone's expression hasn't changed, despite the manhandling, and I think he's too frozen to respond. My insides certainly react, though, and it's all I can do to keep from flicking away the woman's roaming hands. I haven't felt that kind of possessiveness in a long time.

"Sorry, I'm Cameron," I say, hoping to distract myself from doing something unreasonable, and hold out a hand to the unnamed, but very loud, woman. "Boone's an old friend. I haven't seen him in ages, so we have a lot of catching up to do."

The woman's eyes light up. The line moves forward, and she uses the time while I order to look me up and down.

"Did you know each other from CSU? I bet you played football too, huh? It must have been amazing to play on a team with Boone."

I keep the smile plastered on my face despite my internal cringing. If people don't ask me about sports because I'm an African-American male, then they assume because of my size. I was never unathletic, just focused on other things like the debate club and academic decathlon. Those were the competitions I enjoyed.

"Not here," I respond, because it's true enough and I wouldn't be a very good lawyer if I didn't know how to navigate the loopholes. I slide my card and move aside so Boone can go ahead and order.

"Alright, I suppose I'll let you have him this evening," she sighs and says to me as if this poor guy has no say or ownership of his own time. She snags his elbow but he doesn't turn back around. "I'm going to track you down later, Boone. You'll thank me for it."

The ladies leave for the theater, and Boone still has his lips awkwardly grimaced into a smile and his back stiff at attention.

"I think you can relax now. They're gone."

His shoulders drop by an inch, but if he were a dog, I would swear I could still see his hackles up.

"Thanks for the rescue. I couldn't think fast enough."

"No worries. That was the strangest ambush I've ever seen." I grab my Whoppers and stuff them in my jacket pocket before grabbing the popcorn and soda left for me on the counter. "I'm surprised it caught you off guard, though. Women must always be falling all over themselves around you."

Boone shudders, more of his stiffness falling away the longer the woman and her friend are out of sight.

"It's not something I would notice," he says, and I give an internal cheer as the hope that he plays for my team – and it's definitely *not* football – increases. "She's always trying to set me up. I've seen it with the other guys at work too. She's never satisfied. Once they have girlfriends, she pesters them about marriage. Once they get married, she won't stop asking about when they're going to have kids. Then she finds a new guy to harass. Ugh."

Since our hands are full with snacks, I knock his elbow with mine, secretly enjoying even that brief contact. We shift our goodies around to hand our tickets to the attendant and follow his directions down the hall.

"Sorry to ruin your opportunity to prove your self-assurance," he says, making me determined to wheedle more shy teasing from him before the end of the evening.

"I've never been so happy to not be self-assured," I tell him with a grin, stopping just short of winking. "And I don't mind playing along as your old college buddy either, but fair warning. I never played football, so I won't be able to fake it."

"Trust me," he says with a sigh. "I fake it all the time and they never notice."

3

JAY

"Hello, Handsome and Handsomer," I say over the hissing of the espresso machine that Anna works behind me to the two pristinely suited men who approach the register where I work at Espresso Patronum.

"Which one is which?" Kieran asks with a laugh.

"Obviously I'm Handsomer," Cameron says.

Kieran shakes his head. "The man scores one date, and suddenly he's the Don Juan of Fort Collins."

"Wouldn't I have to be straight for that to be an accurate analogy?" Cameron asks.

Kieran turns to me with a huff. "Lawyers."

My insides are churning like the milk that Anna is steaming. "So, you have a date?"

The words don't even sound forced to my ears, but Kieran gives me a curious look.

Right. Because of course Cameron decides to get back out there after a year of being single. Why wouldn't he? And all those hints I've casually tossed out, all that flirting ... why on earth would he have considered me? Not when there's some stranger out there who's probably as built as he is, and not some twig that might snap in two if he thrusts too hard between Cameron's twin paradigms of spherical beauty.

"Where are the muffins? I was hoping for a snack. We were stuck in court all day," Kieran asks as he practically presses his face against the empty bakery display case.

Ah, that explains the suits.

"Unfortunately, the woman who was providing our baked goods moved to Tucson and Larry hasn't found a replacement yet."

"Why don't you bake them here? You've got a kitchen back there," Kieran says because he knows from experience. He's not supposed to go back there, but one night when I was closing and we were going out afterwards, I let him hang out in the back while I finished with the drawer and the locking up.

"I don't know that anyone wants to experience my muffins."

Cameron's smirk makes me replay my words, and I think for the first time ever, I didn't intend the double entendre.

"You're an amazing baker. I think Ted only pretended to like my vegan cookies before you showed me how to perfect them. You should try it."

"I'd be more than happy to experience your muffins if you need a tester." Cameron's wicked grin would normally have me tossing out an equally suggestive retort, but after discovering that he finds me flirty-worthy but not date-worthy, my heart's just not in it. Even that lavender shirt that makes his dark skin glow and my mouth drool can't tempt me into an innuendo duel. So unfair.

"I'll think about it. I'll bring out your drinks in a minute. Go take a load off."

Kieran nods and gives me another concerned look before getting sucked into a discussion with Cameron, nitpicking details about the hearing that I shouldn't be eavesdropping on.

My hands shake as I make their drinks – a spiced Chai for

Cameron's new drink of the day and a tea for Kieran – and I have no idea why. It wasn't like I was expecting Cameron to suddenly decide I was his perfect match and run to me the second he felt ready to date again. I'm not an idiot. I know he's out of my league. But fuck if it doesn't sting, and the realization that I had hoped, so much more than I had even been aware, is wreaking havoc with my motor skills.

I take their drinks to their table, but they barely glance up. I understand. Their work is important. Whereas my work ...

"Congratulations on your date," I tell Cameron. The cup and saucer land so smoothly that it doesn't even slosh against the sides. Kieran's tea, meanwhile, leaves a ring on my tray and on the table in front of him.

"He met him while going to the movies. Alone." Kieran's pointed use of the word mimics the pointed look he gives Cameron over his sip of tea, oblivious to the mess I'm making. I can't believe Cameron actually took my suggestion about the movies. "At first I was mad that he was going to the movies by himself when he has a perfectly good set of friends ready and waiting to hang out at a moment's notice."

My eyebrows rise in an expression of disbelief that Kieran pretends not to notice. Since he and Ted moved in together, it's been like pulling teeth to get either of them from their love nest for a night out.

"But now that I see it was just a ploy to find a man, well, he's forgiven."

Kieran smiles sweetly at Cameron.

"I think you forget, I sign the paychecks," Cameron says, holding his Chai in front of his lips but not taking a sip.

"Nope. Because I remember that I'm indispensable."

"What about you, Jay?" Cameron tilts his head like he's actually curious.

"No, I'm not indispensable."

His frown tugs at things deep in my chest that I didn't know I could still feel.

"I was asking if you'd had any dates recently. Of course you're indispensable. Can you imagine half the people that come into this place if they couldn't get their coffee? You provide a very necessary public service."

I can feel my ears getting hot at his compliment, but I pretend it doesn't faze me. "Nah, they'd just go somewhere else."

"And still be in a mood because they hadn't had you to brighten up their day."

I have no idea what to say to Cameron's sincere-sounding praise. I used to be so much smoother, back when I still had confidence. Now I try to fake it, but genuine compliments still throw me for a loop.

Just as well, I remind myself. No way Cameron is looking for what I'm offering, and even if he was, I'm sure I'm the last place he'd look. I'm most guys' go-to when they want a twinky power bottom, and I regularly leave them disappointed – or worse, laughing – when I explain that I'm a top. Once upon a time, there was a man who brought out the dominant in me like it was the most natural thing for both of us. I thought the skies had opened up and was waiting for the gay angel choir to start singing hymns of BDSM. Instead, I discovered he'd cheated on his boyfriend with me as a side plaything. We were supposed to meet the next day. He had the nerve to show up, all urgent knocking and apologies at the front door, but I pretended I wasn't at home until he finally gave up and went away.

Now, when I need sex, I go to one of the clubs closer to Denver. There's more variety there, and more guys willing to take a chance on me. At least I've got the love of my friends, because I've given up on the idea of having those things – love, sex, friendship – together in one place.

Unlike most regulars, Cameron and Kieran walk their empty

dishes back to the counter instead of leaving them on their table for me to clear later.

"I'll be back tomorrow," Kieran says, and my brain runs through any plans we might have made that I've already forgotten before he adds, "I have more paperwork to file across the street. But when I get here, I'll be expecting muffins."

I shake my head and the ceramic clatter of dishes into the dirty bin masks my sigh. Kieran means well. But Jennifer didn't just make muffins, she made works of art, mixing flavors and textures that I could never hope to compete with. At a place named Espresso Patronum, you expect the baked goods to be magical, not meh. If only Harry Potter could conjure up the perfect muffins for me.

That reminds me of the Harry Potter cookbook my brother and sister-in-law gave me for Christmas a few years back. It was right after I started baking in earnest, and of course they had to use their gift to remind everyone what a dork I had been growing up. I might not bleach it as light now, but I made the perfect Draco growing up, so it sort of became my thing. When Larry bought the old Mugs coffee shop and changed it to Espresso Patronum, adding bookshelves stuffed floor to ceiling, and book-nerd-themed murals on the walls, I felt like I had found my calling. Or maybe not calling but haven, because even though I do make a mean macchiato, it's the place itself that I really love.

Potterverse muffins would be fun, though. Butterbeer, treacle tart, pumpkin pasties ... I might play around with some muffin ideas after all. Not that I'm bringing them to the store, mind you. But I could let Kieran, maybe even Cameron, give them a test.

Since I opened this morning, I bike home at a reasonable four o'clock. Plenty of time to bake, especially if I ignore the baby blanket I'm knitting for my soon-to-be niece or nephew that taunts me from my knitting basket in the corner of my living room.

I toss my jean jacket onto the sofa and roll the stress from my shoulders. It may not be to everyone's liking, but my living room, which might as well be a museum of my various crafting phases, is the only place where I can truly relax. The comfy armchair and sofa, both covered in crocheted rainbow blankets. Overhead hang potted plants in various states of death, though I really do try to keep them alive, snug in knitted cozies dangling from macramé hangers. My one attempt at art – a collage of photographs of my family's dog Coco highlighted by oil paint and fabrics to give it texture and relief – covers the wall behind the sofa. The old coffee table benefitted, kind of, from my learning how to decoupage, and is covered with photos of studly men from the forties and fifties, like Rock Hudson, Gregory Peck, and Cary Grant.

I pull out my notepad from the junk drawer of my kitchen and start to brainstorm. Butterbeer and treacle muffins would be pretty similar unless I can come up with other combinations to set them apart. Pumpkin muffins are a given, but I need to somehow spice them up. And I need a chocolate offering, too. Cookbooks begin to pile up on my counter, left open or Post-It notes sticking out from pages, until I finally have three recipes that I think will complement each other, yet offer enough variety and HP charm to work with the coffee shop's theme. Not that I'm baking for the coffee shop.

I list out the ingredients I need and rummage through my cabinets and drawers, crossing off items I already have. Thankfully, the grocery store around the corner has everything I need, and I'm back in my crafting sweatpants – that I will otherwise never admit to anyone that I wear, but they are so comfy when baking or knitting that I refuse to feel guilty – and in the kitchen in no time.

Only for Us

If I were going to do the baking for Espresso Patronum, I think I've put together a nice eclectic regular mix, then there could be a weekly or monthly seasonal special. The treacle and apple muffins are the first in the oven, and the whole apartment smells divine. There's an old mustard container in the fridge that really should have been thrown away weeks ago when I opened a new one, so I take it out and hand wash it so that I can use it for the caramel drizzle. Waste not and all that.

My hands are too sticky now to work on the baby blanket between bakes, so I mix up the pumpkin-zucchini-chocolate chip muffins and set them aside. They might not fill the apartment with the same heavenly scent, but a quick dip of my pinky tells me they taste just as good. Maybe even better, if that subtle spiced heat from fall breads is more your thing than a summery apple pie.

In between the pumpkin muffins and the final batch, I throw one of those instant soups into the microwave so that I have some actual food in my stomach and not just raw muffin batter. The recipes make two dozen of each, so I have forty-eight beautiful muffin babies cooling on every possible inch of available counter space, and I eat my soup from a mug that I don't dare put down in the middle of my chaos.

After the final butterbeer muffins with a brown sugar and pecan streusel topping come out of the oven, I've had to start packing away the first set of muffins into plastic containers, just to have more room. I leave a couple out so that I can take pictures of all three varieties together on a pretty crystal cake pedestal. I post the pic to Instagram and sigh at my mess. All the fun bits are done, and I'm exhausted, but I can't leave this mess until tomorrow.

The baby blanket still taunts me. At this rate, the child will be headed to college and the blanket will barely cover his or her thigh before I finish it.

My phone dings with a notification, and Kieran's comment scrolls along the top of my phone.

"If I don't get one of each, I'm staging a revolt," Kieran writes under my picture. "#gimmemuffins."

To my surprise, there was another comment ahead of his, from username CamMac.

"#muffintester. #experiencejaysmuffins."

My laugh turns into a groan as I grab the sponge and get to work cleaning. I'll set aside one of each for both of them, and then probably drop the rest off at the rescue mission. What was I thinking, making this many muffins? My apartment is #muffin-explosion.

4

BOONE

"You had better get your head out of your ass, Boone," Buzz Superczynski, the GM of our dealership, sprays as he leans both hands against the front of my desk. "If your numbers don't pick up by next week, you won't even make the top three, much less the top seller for the month. What the hell's the matter with you lately?"

The sales associates' desks create a straight line in the center of the sales floor, glass fronts and sides, with the only solid wall at our backs. Which means if I look to my left or to my right, I could see that every associate here is watching Buzz chew my ass for my lack of focus this month. Most of them watch with horror, but this kind of motivational speech is second nature to me. Buzz is just another in a long line of coaches, and the tactics he uses, frankly, are comforting and familiar. If I had a boss who coddled me, I'm not sure how I'd respond – probably cry like a baby.

"Sorry, sir. I'm on top of it."

I am, actually. I've been emailing several customers and one, the wife of a local businessman, has an appointment this afternoon. She wants the latest SUV, and so far, all of her correspondence has been about colors and features. I don't think price is a factor. I should be in the top three by the end of the day, and my streak of top seller for ten months in a row still safely within reach. I might not love being a car salesman, but I can't ignore the lure of a competition.

"Don't let it happen again. You're here because the ladies love you, and the men want to reminisce with you. But if you think for a second that you're not replaceable, think again."

Oh, I know full well I'm replaceable. Even on the field, after my knee surgery, I was replaceable in an instant. Even though I was a perfect patient and stayed off it, despite my dad's constant berating, I still needed surgery. After that, it never was the same. They let me back on the field, but by then, a newer, hotter, healthier version had already taken my place. Nobody cared about my eighty-yard throw when my legs had lost their full range of motion.

Buzz is right, though. I need to get my head back in the game. Ever since seeing Alison at the movies last weekend, I've been off. Excited, because I have a date with the gorgeous man who came to my rescue, but even that can't overpower the creepy feeling from the movies. Not like I think Alison is stalking me, but that she's noticing me, and I don't want to be on display. She's talked to me more this week than she has in the entire time I've worked here. I knew she was nosy, but she seems to think that running into me in public means that suddenly she has a right to all of my business. I survived nosy reporters in college by keeping my head down and my life private. I continued out of habit, and I'm not about to let her ruin that.

I really don't want her in my business.

I click on the bookmark set to Cameron MacGowan, Attorney at Law. I should be preparing for three o'clock SUV lady, but I much more enjoy staring at the dark brown eyes of the first man in ages who tempted me to out myself – at least enough to ask for a first, or is it maybe the second, date. He put me at ease in a way that I've never felt before, and that was even more tempting than his GQ attractiveness.

We sat together at the movies since Alison and her friend were only a few rows ahead of us and could look back at any time. Which she did. Often. He introduced himself, keeping his voice low so Alison wouldn't catch on, and slid his business card to me before we left. He was the perfect movie companion. I easily get pissed off by talking during movies because it makes it hard for me to focus.

We chatted a little before and a little after. Enough for me to guess that he was interested. When I texted him the next day to see if he wanted to join me for dinner on Friday, I got an immediate yes. If I had actually been holding my breath, instead of feeling like I had, I would have been fine. Good to know I wasn't so out of practice that I couldn't read the signals. I haven't initiated that kind of step, well, ever. In college, it just sort of happened, and I haven't tried to date since ruining the only decent relationship I've ever had with Arthur.

Now I just have to worry about the fact that I have a date. With a man. Out in public. I decide going to the pool side of the local pub is the best choice. We can eat and drink and maybe shoot some pool. Even after my bum knee, I kept in shape, so I'll take any excuse to bend over and show off my ass. The move has worked well enough for me in the past.

By the time Friday arrives, I've talked myself into a fake sense of calm. My jeans are tight, my shirt a slim-fitting button-down that emphasizes my broad shoulders without screaming "date." We'll look like two buddies getting together for a guys' night. Perfect.

McGillicutty's Pub takes less than two minutes to drive and only five to walk. There's an internal debate over walking and drinking versus looking my best when I show up, but I'm not going to get sweaty from a five-minute walk in perfect April weather. The sun still glows over the horizon, and the light breeze means I'll be cool and dry and fashionable with wind-blown hair when I arrive. I laugh to myself – I haven't put this much thought into my appearance in I don't know how long.

I don't see Cameron when I first enter, so I scope out a booth in the back near a pool table. Five minutes, then ten, go by, and my cold beer gets too warm from my hands worrying around the glass. I probably look like a tennis official, with my constant swiveling to the door and back. At fifteen minutes, I give in and take my phone out from my back pocket and send him a text.

Boone: I got us a table. I'm near the last pool table.

Cameron: I'm in the wrong place, then, because there are no pool tables here.

A bead of sweat trickles from my brow as the fear I didn't realize had started to collect in my belly suddenly flies away. He's in the wrong part of the restaurant. I'm not being stood up. Oh, thank God.

Boone: There are two buildings for McGillicutty's. You're in the restaurant one. I'm in the fun one

Cameron: Well heaven forbid I not have fun. I'll be right over.

I watch the door like a hawk and stand and wave the second Cameron enters, ignoring the fact that my dopey grin ruins my carefully constructed cool. His dark blue trousers emphasize his long legs – and probably his ass, although he hasn't turned around yet for me to see – and his light blue shirt has the sleeves casually rolled up to expose forearms with muscles that twitch with obvious strength. My mouth is as dry as the Sahara as I take him in from head to toe.

"Hey, there you are," he says warmly, and it matches his smile. I've been so entranced with his approach that my brain has stalled.

"Wow," I say, wincing internally that I couldn't come up with something more eloquent. I've been labelled a dumb jock my whole life, despite the fact that I enjoyed school and did well in all classes, not just the athletic ones.

Cameron's smile stretches impossibly wider, like he's trying not to laugh at me, but the heat from his eyes lets me know it wouldn't be mean, even if he wasn't able to hold it back.

"I forgot about this place."

"I thought it would be fun. Low key." I shrug before noticing I've sucked in my lower lip, a nervous habit. Biting would be next but I force myself to relax and smile instead; however, I'm pretty sure it has the unintended side effect of making me look twitchy, as Cameron schools his smile to a normal size.

He notices my empty bottle, the beer I sucked down between minutes ten and fifteen, the span of time it took for me to go from confident to sad-sack when I believed he had stood me up.

"I'm going to grab a drink. Want a refill?"

"That would be great, thanks."

I try not to drink too much. I'm still so used to measuring and counting everything I put in my body that it's a difficult habit to break. But it's helping my nerves, so I'll have one more. For luck.

Cameron returns with a beer for me and a whiskey sour for himself. The menus are stashed between condiments on the table, and when he's picked out his dinner, I flag the waitress over to take our orders. We both try wood-fired pizza, although mine is covered in the works while Cameron orders a simple Margherita.

My leg bounces under the table, probably because all I can think is how lucky I am that he's here with me. Every time I catch myself, I stop and glance to see if he's noticed. If he has, he's being polite and pretending not to notice that I'm a nervous wreck.

Unfortunately, even if I wasn't stretched so tight, my ability to small talk begins and ends with the weather and his job. Thankfully, he's able to take the lead, and talks about how happy he is now that he's opened up his own practice here in Fort Collins. When he mentions that he's originally from California, I'm not surprised. He holds himself with a certain sophistication and confidence that screams big city. I ask what type of cases he takes, and his passion overflows as he talks about helping LGBT people with civil rights issues. I confess to myself that I'm a little starry-eyed.

When I was the star QB of the CSU Rams, I was often on the receiving end of such looks. I had talent, not denying that, combined with good genes and a work ethic ramped into overdrive. Still, maybe it's my mom's influence, but I always looked up to people who changed the world – the guy who took his millions and started the shoe project for the homeless in Denver or the lady who started the nonprofit that provided meals during the summer for kids who otherwise wouldn't have food when school was out of session. Those people took their talents and made the world a better place. I miss the days when I had loftier goals than top seller at Super Motors.

I love football. I love being part of a team, being a part of something. And I do think it makes you a better person, in that you learn how to work well with others, that success hinges on it, and that the things you do affect others. It's why I always wanted to pass the opportunity on to others. But it's not like the equivalence of sainthood or winning the Nobel Peace Prize or something. Like sure, Al Pacino is the greatest actor alive, but does that make him a better person than the rest of us? Hell, even a good person? I have no idea. But if he is, it isn't because of his acting talent, but what he did for others because of it.

I had dreams when I was still at CSU that I would start a nonprofit for kids, some sort of summer sports camp for those that wouldn't otherwise be able to afford any kind of summer camp, much less one taught by college stars, or hopefully NFL stars. That dream vanished along with my football career, but I still haven't lost that desire to make the world better somehow. Selling overpriced cars sure as hell isn't it.

"Sorry," he says with a short laugh that indicates he's embarrassed about something. Probably my drooling. "I sort of hijacked that conversation."

"I don't mind. You're *fascinating*," I say, then realize how dorky and fawning I sound, and suddenly my napkin is very, very interesting. My fingers shred through it as I try to distract myself from saying something even worse.

"Want to play?" I risk a glance, and he nods over at the pool table. I think I could fall in love right now. Everyone always assumes being a star quarterback, or former one, means I'm loaded with confidence. And I am, about some things. But I'm so out of my league with Cameron, yet over and over, he does or says exactly the right thing to put me at ease again. "I'll rack 'em, you break 'em."

I nod like a bobblehead on crack. Cameron bent over the table. Yes, please.

I watch Cameron walk away to get the balls from the bartender. Twin tapers hang perfectly from each side, clinging to the curve of his ass and falling down slim legs. If his forearms are any indication, he might be slim, but he's incredibly fit. I wonder what he does to work out. Maybe we could start working out together. And maybe I could stop getting ahead of myself and make it through this date first.

His leg kicks up onto a rung of one of the barstools, pushing his butt out farther. What I wouldn't give to be able to worship that ass.

He returns just before our pizzas and stops in the middle of racking up the balls to ask our waitress for a set of silverware.

"Tell me you're not one of those guys who eats their pizzas with a knife and fork."

"If by 'those guys' you mean men who would rather not lay waste to their nice slacks or get the nasty germs they probably just collected from those pool balls into their food and end up hospitalized with some nasty funk, then I am happily one of 'those guys.'"

I laugh and hold up my hands in surrender. "You win. Now for the rest of the night, you're going to be wary of my hands, and that is not how I wanted this evening to go."

"There's this magical place called a restroom, where we can wash our hands after playing pool."

I pick at my first slice of pizza, not willing to stop our fun bantering with a mouthful of food.

"I've heard of showering together but not handwashing together. It doesn't sound quite as fun, but I'm willing to give it a try."

Cameron stands in front of me with a pool cue outstretched. "I like a man that's willing to try for me."

I'm surprised I don't land face-first on the floor – death by flirting.

I'm good at pool. I swear, I really am. But that darkly intense stare has heat pouring over me until I fumble my stick and scratch. The other balls barely shuffle, but the cue ball sails smoothly into the side pocket.

"You're easily rattled," Cameron says while smothering his grin. "That is handy information to file away for later."

I'm a former college quarterback and once upon a time potential NFL draft pick, for fuck's sake. I am not easily rattled. I want to be affronted, but my insides are still too wobbly to do anything but agree with the man as he leans against his stick and gives me a long and obvious perusal.

Maybe it's nerves. Maybe I'm shaky from not having

anything but a couple of beers in my stomach, so I take the opportunity to sit and eat a slice. Cameron leans down, pretending to assess the angles as he determines where to position the cue ball, but really, I know he's trying – and succeeding – to wind me up even more.

Well, two can play at that game.

I finish my slice and wipe down my greasy hands on a napkin, then finish the final swallow of my beer. Cameron takes his first shot and sinks two solids. He walks around the table, finding his next shot, and when he bends down to take it, I position myself directly across from him.

My pants are already tight, but watching him parade his perfect ass around has me chubbed up to half-mast. When Cameron looks across to line up his shot, he's met with an eyeful. His cue bounces off the table and the cue ball skips into the air, coming to a slow stop as it softly clinks the seven ball it was aimed at.

"Hmm," I say and pretend to tap my finger against my chin in thought as I press my hips further against the table, making the outline of my package even more obvious. "It looks like you're easily rattled. Good to know."

Cameron barks a laugh that probably has the attention of the entire pub, but I can't take my eyes off him to find out. He stalks around the table and boxes me in, one hand clutching the rim of the table and the other holding the cue stick against the edge on either side of me. I can feel him press against me. With the thin fabric of his trousers, I'm surprised I hadn't noticed him before, because he feels hard and thick against my ass.

My eyes shutter closed and I take deep breaths, trying to get myself under control in public. He's so fucking hot, and I bet he'd be even hotter taking control in the bedroom. The thought almost has me at full mast, right there, until I open my eyes and see Alison standing on the other side of the table.

Her pink blouse looks silky and soft, and her hair is done up in a ponytail that curls under before it hits her neck. Her friend from the movies, I can't remember her name at the moment, looks almost identical, but in green.

"Boone!" Alison waves and smiles sweetly, as if she hadn't just caught me rubbing off against a pool table. Her wicked eyes tell a different story, though. "And your friend ... Cameron, right? I had no idea you were going to be here."

Cameron's body doesn't relent from caging me in, but as he leans down to whisper in my ear, it gives the impression of room and I gulp air like I've been starved of it all night.

"Does this woman stalk you or something? It's kind of creepy."

Creepy indeed. And worrying, given that it looks like Cameron is about to fuck me over the top of this pool table.

I squirm out from under him and force a laugh. "Cameron was just teaching me how to play pool. Twenty-six years old; you'd think I'd have learned by now."

I can tell by the way Alison is sizing us up that she doesn't buy it, but her sidekick Sonia seems to. "I can teach you," Sonia says to me with a wink that makes my skin crawl. "We had a table at our sorority."

Of course they did.

"Uh, yeah. Totally," I say and try to pretend my voice hasn't crept into Mickey Mouse territory.

"Well, since you've learned your lesson," Cameron says with an even voice, "I'm going to head on home. Lots of options on a Friday night that are better than teaching your *friend* to play pool."

My heart sinks at the way he practically spits the word "friend."

"Right?" Alison says, waving her hand in the air like maybe

there's some invisible fly she's shooing away. Everything about this woman is a mystery to me. "What was Boone thinking?"

She doesn't get an answer, as Cameron takes his food up to the bar and I watch in befuddlement as the bartender slides it into a box and Cameron slaps down some bills.

"Oh well. You could always join Sonia and me over at the restaurant."

I look at Alison like she has grown a mouse-sized wart on her forehead.

What the fuck just happened?

5

CAMERON

I don't know where my head is right now. It's been four days since that disastrous date, and I still can't stop replaying it in my mind. Everything was perfect until his work friend showed up, but then I had to go back and rethink everything about the whole date with that lens in place.

The evening might have been something I'd just as easily do with friends – pizza, pool, and beer – but the teasing wasn't. God, the way those jeans showed off every feature like fondant on a cake. And the eager but shy looks he kept dropping made me freer with my own teases – bending over the pool table and showing off my ass. It was fun and lighthearted, the perfect first date after so many long months of closing myself off to happiness.

Dylan and I hadn't had the perfect relationship. No one does, if they're being honest. We met my final year of college, when he was thirty, and I thought he hung the moon. He was the most beautiful man in any club, and he could have had anyone, but he wanted me. He stuck with me through law school, but he always wanted to keep our lives separate. We were boyfriends, and yes, I spent most nights with him. But while he was careful never to get too close, I clung, desperate to stay in his orbit. I always figured Ted was the reason for that.

Kieran's Ted.

Life is funny, if you're not too jaded to laugh at yourself.

Ted and Dylan were long-term boyfriends from high school through their twenties. Their formative years. I couldn't compete with that, though God knows I tried. I let Dylan drag me out night after night. I'm more of a homebody, but he longed to be admired. He chased the excitement of nights out, dancing, clubs, and drinking. Dylan could make me laugh like no one else, and the way his eyes roamed over my body could strike a fire under me in seconds flat. He was the sun and I was Mercury, orbiting as close as I could without completely burning up. I never could shake the feeling that I simply wasn't enough for him. I don't think anyone but Ted would have been.

For a few months now, I've been starting to think I was ready to get back out there. Not with someone bright and shining and dangerous like Dylan. If I wanted that, I'd have taken Jay up on all his flirtatious banter ages ago. That little firecracker of a man is exactly my type – full of life and gorgeous – and fully aware of it. No, I'm not ready for someone like Jay. But a nice guy that I met while out – handsome, funny, sweet – sounded like the perfect way to ease myself back into the dating scene without having my heart squeeze with constant reminders of Dylan.

It was a perfect plan, until that man ended up freaking out over someone seeing me touch him in public. I have never been in the closet in my life, and I don't intend to start now.

Kieran raps on my door while sticking his head inside at the same time.

"Your two o'clock is here."

"Thanks," I say while digging through my drawer, trying to find my favorite gel pen. I take hand notes during initial client meetings so I can focus on our face-to-face interactions. I think

Only for Us

I'm pretty good at reading people, at least before last Friday. Plus, it's just rude to sit there and type on a computer while you're talking with a client, especially when they are often upset when they first get here. By the second or third meeting, they've progressed to pissed-the-hell-off. But initially, it's shock and sadness that is the overwhelming emotion we get to process together.

"Hi."

The smooth tenor rolls over me like toasted marshmallow or a worn but cozy robe. I recognize the voice that lulled me into a false sense of comfort on Friday, and I'm not surprised to see him hesitate to take the chair in front of me.

"Hi," I reply, taking a secret pleasure in watching Boone's fingers pick nervously at the detailing on the top of the chair.

His words spill out like he's been collecting and memorizing them, and he can't wait to be rid of them.

"I'm sorry for freaking out on you Friday. I didn't mean to make you feel like I was embarrassed to be seen with you."

Apparently, my sadism has its limits, or maybe Boone is simply incredibly effective with his apologies, but I can feel my anger begin to bleed away.

"You don't need to explain yourself," I say with less hostility than I still feel. "Are you here just to apologize or is there something else?"

"I was fired from my job yesterday. I'd like to hire you," he says to my surprise. At first, he's still unable to look me in the eye, until he finally raises his head and adds, "And I do need to explain myself."

"Please, have a seat." Yes, I was mad before, but honestly, I would never withhold help from someone in need.

He sits, but his legs bounce on the balls of his feet, like he's ready to bolt and run at a moment's notice.

"I don't really have an excuse for why I've stayed in the closet all these years. At least not a good one. Between football and my father, especially back when it seemed like I was destined for the NFL, I always assumed a love life was something I would never have."

Maybe I should have done more homework on Boone, but I had no idea he had a real shot at playing professionally. Playing college ball could mean any number of things, and rarely a professional career. That right there explains so much. Even these days, with more and more celebrities and athletes coming out and braving the spotlight, being gay can be a nail in the coffin for any career.

Still, I say a little weakly, "There are out football players."

I expect him to laugh or scoff, but the sadness that infects his expression erases the remains of my anger.

"Right. They probably have supportive parents and brilliant backup plans. I had Silas Boone the First and a job as a car salesman. Now I know I wouldn't have even had the sales job had it been my coming-out plan B. Alison shared what she saw Friday night with the entire break room first thing yesterday morning. Not thirty minutes later, I get called in for a meeting with my boss, where he informs me that I'm just not Super Motors material."

It's a tale I've heard time and again, only the details change. I started out working at a large firm in California after graduating from law school. Granted, we weren't doing LGBT civil and employment cases, but I heard the stories often enough anyway. Now I'm practicing in Colorado, a state where we elected the first openly gay governor, and this shit is still happening. A different person might feel defeated. Thankfully, my momma raised a fighter.

My hand pauses on my notepad where I've jotted down a few questions for later.

"Anyway." Boone clears his throat and I glance up, realizing I had gotten lost in my thoughts and zoned out while staring at my pen. So much for my excellent face-to-face abilities. "I just wanted to let you know how sorry I am for making you feel bad, or like I was ashamed. You're amazing, like a real-world Superman. If anything, you should have been ashamed of slumming it with me."

I set down my pen and look him straight in the eye.

"We'll tackle your job here in a second. For now, I'm just Cameron," I say, wishing I could slide around the desk and take his hand. I'm not sure where the boundaries are at this point, though, so I stay seated and school my hands to be content clasping each other in my lap. "We're okay. Did it feel shitty to have you bolt the second someone noticed us together? Yes, but my job is living proof that being true to yourself and paying your bills aren't always complementary creatures. In an ideal world, it wouldn't make any difference. But in the real world, coming out has consequences. I do know that, and I should have remembered it."

For the first time since entering my office, Boone's shoulders drop the tension they've been carrying.

"Yeah. After my accident and losing my spot on the team, I thought about coming out." Okay, I really need to Google this man, because there's obviously a big backstory that probably all college football fans know, but I'm totally clueless about it. "But my dad was already so disappointed in me, I didn't want to make things worse. I kept my head down and worked my ass off to get an academic scholarship since I lost my sports one. I still have some student loans, but not as much. By the time I graduated and got the job at the dealership, I had no life to speak of anyway, so I kept quiet. Buzz and all the staff acted like I was still some big deal, and it felt like old habits, just letting everyone believe what they wanted."

"Coming out is a personal decision, and no one should make

it for you. I'm sorry I reacted badly. I didn't even consider that you weren't out, given how obvious I thought we were being."

Boone's cheeks brighten. "Yeah. I liked that."

The fact that I've turned him from nervous wreck to shyly proud fills me with more confidence, as well as the desire to test the waters again.

"It's been a long time since I've been on a date. I've never been in the closet, so I will admit that my gut reaction was that I'd been slapped in the face. I should have been more understanding. I just got so caught up in you. Frankly, I was having so much fun, I forgot myself."

"Yeah?"

"Indeed. So. Maybe we could try it again sometime? Now that I know you're not out–"

"Well, I am now," Boone says, punctuated with an adorable arm flail, like he's throwing in the towel.

"Then we should definitely try it again sometime," I say, trying to tamp down my grin. "Let you see how nice it is to actually go out on a date-like date with a guy."

"Yeah, I'd like that."

"Good. Now, about your job ..."

I should have thought this through a little better, because now I'm so excited, I doubt I can make it through an hour of work talk. Maybe I can excuse myself and go do the Snoopy happy dance outside the door where he won't see me acting like a giddy fool.

~

Jay moves efficiently behind the counter, one of the many things I find so attractive about him. His confidence and style. His ability to tackle almost anything and make it look effortless. Of course those pillowy red lips set against his lovely, milky skin always ping at my heart. Maybe I'm a coward for picking the guy I think is safer for my heart, but then again, after our meeting on Tuesday, maybe my heart isn't safe either way.

Jay sees me lingering at the door and gives a wave. His smile is so bright it propels me forward.

"Hmm, I wonder what I should make you today. How's your day been? Good?" he asks, and I feel the strength of his charm aimed at me.

"Great," I answer with a hundred-watt smile. I can't help them around Jay. I glance to the bakery counter and back. "Still no muffins?"

Jay sighs.

The bakery case is woefully empty, but Kieran and I did as much pushing as I think Jay would allow. His muffins were what I'd imagine being served in heaven, but the man could not be convinced to offer them in the bakery. It's disturbing to see Jay not confident in something, especially an area where he most definitely should be.

"It's criminal, you know. Keeping us from them when you could be sharing your gifts with the world. Perhaps I'll sue."

Jay's lips twist as he turns his back to me to make my surprise drink.

"And what good would that do?" he tosses over his shoulder. "A judge might order me to turn over the recipe, but it takes skill to make those muffins."

I lean onto the counter with a predatory grin. Teasing Jay should not be so much fun.

"Oh, I can imagine the skills you possess in those hands. Perhaps it would go to mediation instead. I could convince the mediator that a sufficient compromise would be you making the muffins for me instead of turning over the recipe."

Jay returns with my coffee and leans forward, showing me he's not the kind to back down.

"Compromise, huh? And what would I be getting out of it?"

"My eternal adoration, of course."

Jay shakes his head and heads to the register, which chimes in sync with the front door bells. Boone enters, his cheeks flushed and his hair messy from the wind. Okay, so it's bad form to flirt with another guy while you're waiting for your date. My head knows this. My heart just wants to wrap them both up and hoard them like a dragon.

Foolish heart. You haven't even recovered from losing Dylan, and already you're shoving me in the path of not one, but two men who have the capacity to completely break you.

It's like I'm a teenager all over again. I never could focus on just one crush. I had to fall for one guy's smile and another's talent and another's generosity. Dylan demanded so much of my attention, maybe I only thought my indecisiveness was cured.

"In that case," Jay says, grabbing my card with a wink, "I'm sure an arrangement ca ..."

I follow Jay's eyes as his words trail off into nothing, and he stares wide-eyed at the man who has wrapped a tender arm around my waist. A man, I now notice, wearing a mirror copy of that shocked expression.

6

BOONE

There are no words for the tsunami in my stomach. Christ, this week is going to kill me. It's almost enough to tempt me to throw my hands up, go home, and bury under a blanket for the next month.

When I went to Cameron's work yesterday, I could only hope he'd help me with my work claim. The fact that he forgave me for my stupidity and wanted to see me again was more than I thought possible. But once again, fate has decided to have a laugh at my expense, because standing right in front of us is the only man I've never been able to get out of my head.

He has a gold nametag pinned to his brown apron. Jay. For anyone who didn't know him, the name might suit him. He seems a flighty, dainty thing. But those people haven't been underneath him, trapped by his dominance and pinned by his eyes that look like Earth from afar, a mesmerizing mix of greens and blues. Those eyes are pinning me right now.

"Jay, sorry," Cameron says, glancing between us. "I should introduce you. This is Silas."

"Boone," I correct. I hate being called Silas. I only told

Cameron my full name for legal purposes. Silas is my father, and especially now, it makes me cringe.

"And Boone, this is Jay. If you're looking for the best espresso or the best pair of muffins," Cameron says with a wink, "look no further."

Did he just ...

Before I can wrap my brain around what Cameron meant by that comment, he ducks his head like he's embarrassed himself and asks me what I'd like.

"Just a regular coffee, splash of milk. Thanks."

"Go sit," Jay commands and I feel it in my dick. "I'll bring it out to you."

Cameron pulls out a chair for me, and I plump even more. Shit, it's so wrong to be turned on by two guys on a single date. My brain is buzzing and my pants are tight. Thank God Jay sets a coffee down in front of me almost immediately, so at least I have something to do with my hands.

Cameron's fighting a laugh at my fidgeting.

"It kind of looked like you and Jay might already know each other."

I think that's putting it mildly, but at least he says it like he's curious and not accusing.

"Um, yeah, we hooked up once a long time ago."

"You obviously made a big impression on each other, for so long ago." He smiles then reaches over to still my hands on my coffee mug. "I'm not trying to be snarky, I promise. He's an attractive man. You'd have to be blind not to appreciate it."

The warmth of his hands and the gentleness of his eyes encourage me to be honest. This is a topic that's almost as difficult for me to discuss as being gay.

"It wasn't only that."

I pause, trying to figure out how best to put it. Should I just blurt it out?

Only for Us

"Okay, now I'm curious," he says, and his hand, which hasn't left mine, encourages me with a little squeeze.

"Let's just say, I used to be a quarterback in football, but sexually my position would be wide receiver."

His dark lips quiver and his teeth bite down on his rosy lower lip for a split second before giving in to a grin.

"Not tight end?"

"Well, maybe that too," I say, not minding the joke for the first time. If I'm going to be honest, I might as well go all in. I really like Cameron, so I guess it's best to get it all out there now. "But to have this little guy be so toppy and bossy, it was the hottest thing I've ever done. So far."

I can see Cameron's eyes flare with heat and I breathe a quiet sigh of relief. It looks like my honesty turned him on. Maybe I'll have to go into more detail later when we're alone. God, please let us go somewhere alone later. It's awkward as fuck having this conversation with Jay standing right over there. My eyes flit to the counter and he turns away, pretending he wasn't watching us.

Cameron takes a sip of his drink and speaks as if he isn't undressing me with his eyes or imagining Jay topping me. It's impressive, but he did sort of go to school for it. I wouldn't have much confidence in his lawyering abilities if he lost his cool so easily.

"What happened? You guys were polite just now, but I'm getting the impression it didn't necessarily end amicably."

"Worse. Fuck. How is it that we're dragging all my shitty history out and it's only, what, our second date?"

"I won't judge."

"You say that, but once it's out there in the world, you can't help but think of me differently. Hell, I do."

He pins me with a look that's almost as effective as Jay's, and

I find my mouth opening and the words spilling out before I can stop them.

"I had a boyfriend at the time. A guy who was sweet and didn't mind, or at least suffered through, our relationship staying in the closet. I was young and so fucking full of myself. I didn't deserve him. Either of them. Anyway, Jay and I just sort of happened one day, but then my boyfriend found out and, well, I deserved what I got. Which was nothing. Neither one would have anything to do with me after that. Not that I blame them."

Cameron's hand returns to mine.

"We've all done stupid things when we were younger. Things we regret. It's what we do from there, how we make amends and choose to be better that matters."

"Well then, I'm still a fucking failure. I never apologized to either one of them. I didn't turn my life around or become a better person. I became a car salesman, for fuck's sake. And as my mom always says, 'Once a cheater, always a cheater.'"

"And as my mom always said, 'There's nothing a little forgiveness won't fix.'" His look brooks no argument, but my emotions have been put in a Cameron blender and all that's left is a puddle of warm goo.

How can he still look at me like I'm a creamy caramel sundae he wants to dive headfirst into? It's taken me a long time to stop actively punishing myself for my mistake back then. Staying single and celibate was part of it, because I was afraid to make the same mistake again. But I've never forgiven myself, probably because I know neither Arthur nor Jay could have either.

Yet here's a man, a good man, willing to take a chance on me. It's so much more than I deserve.

"Are you done with your coffee?" he asks, his voice suddenly deeper than it has been before.

I nod like a fool.

"Then let's take this back to my place."

Only for Us

More nodding, but my tongue is suddenly glued to my mouth as my brain short-circuits.

Cameron again helps me with my chair, which I probably shouldn't find so swoony, but there it is. I risk a look back and my eyes meet Jay's. He plasters on a smile that looks as sincere as Buzz's on his bus bench ads and waves.

"Bye, Jay," Cameron calls, because his eyes don't miss a thing. "I'll see you tomorrow, and I'll want to try your muffins."

Jay's fake smile drops and his eyes widen. Yeah, there wasn't any mistaking it that time, yet I'm not jealous. If anything, I find it interesting that Cameron finds us both attractive, although I admittedly find both him and Jay attractive. You couldn't have a more physically polar opposite pair, and their personalities are also so different, yet I still find both men completely alluring.

"Go there often?" I ask while trying not to shiver from the hand at my back. He guides me down the sidewalk to his car, a ruby Prius that I can tell is the latest model.

"It's my office manager's favorite spot. He got me hooked."

I wonder if it has more to do with the blond pixie behind the counter than the coffee, but I can hardly blame him for his heated looks at Jay when I'm sure I looked similarly smitten. That, and I know how good it feels to be on the receiving end of those looks. Surely Jay deserves that feeling as much as I do.

"Is that how you know Jay?"

"No, although it's still through my office manager, Kieran. They're buddies, so he comes into the office a lot. And I've had dinner with Kieran and his boyfriend when we've both been invited. A friend of a friend kind of thing. He's certainly full of life."

Cameron frowns at that, which I don't understand, but don't feel confident enough to ask about. There are still so many mysteries that remain unanswered. Like why is he still single when Jay would obviously jump at the chance to go out with him? He mentioned that he hadn't dated in a long time but didn't say why. It's curious, but the last thing I'd want to do is pressure him.

What a weird beginning to a relationship, if that's where this thing with Cameron is going. I certainly hope so. His nature isn't just kind and considerate, it's warm and lovely, and just a little possessive. No, he doesn't try to dominate me, but his self-assured care makes me feel good, which is such a strange thing to think about someone I've only recently met. It's not love at first sight, or even lust. It's connection. Like a molecular bond.

"Where'd you go?" he asks, and I realize that I've been zoning out the window, lost in wistful thoughts of possibility when I ought to stay more grounded.

"Sorry. Just lost in thought. It's been a while for me."

"Me too."

Cameron's hand clasps mine and holds it tight for the rest of the drive to his place. Sex, I've done. Making out in the back of Tommy LaRue's Volvo senior year, check. But this simple act of holding hands, whether in public or privately, just for us, is entirely new. It sounds ridiculous that such a small gesture means so much, but it sets the squirming in my belly at ease, replacing anxiety with anticipation.

At least until we arrive at his condo, which is tall windows and glassed-in fireplace walls and makes me suddenly self-conscious about my jeans and t-shirt. I met him after work, so I didn't worry when I spotted him in his perfectly fitted trousers and silk tie. But in this space, that looks so much classier than I could ever imagine being, I feel like a charlatan.

"It's just a rental," Cameron says, oblivious to my distress. Or maybe he thinks I'm judging, though I can't imagine any negative comments about this place. "I'm hoping to buy, eventually. I just wanted to get a better idea of the area before I made a decision."

"That makes sense," I say, forcing my feet forward after kicking off my shoes by the front door. Even the floors shine, and I don't want to be the one to ruin them. "I've lived in the same little apartment on the west side of town for five years now, but I can't imagine living anywhere else. I tend to be set in my ways, as long as my basic needs are met."

"I can think of some of your basic needs I'd like to meet," Cameron says, hooking a finger through one of my belt loops and waggling his eyebrows at me. I can't help but burst out laughing.

"That was truly terrible."

"It was. I'll admit it. You should feel bad for me and try to make me feel better."

My head shakes but I can't stop the smile from spreading across my face.

This goofy man is why none of the rest of this, the clothes and the view, matters. Because he doesn't let it.

If I hadn't already felt myself falling, that would have been the final push.

7

CAMERON

The expression on Boone's face, like I'm everything, almost has me calling the whole thing off. This was supposed to be just a bit of fun, ease me back into dating, not rival or replace my relationship with Dylan. I can't begin to piece apart how that makes me feel, but I also can't disappoint Boone now that he's here. I'm sure most people take one look at his *Men's Health* magazine-cover body and miss the man's fragility, but I can tell he's one rejection away from cracking apart.

My hand moves from his belt loop to cup his cheek, warm and a little scratchy with shadow. His eyes close as he leans into it and I take the opportunity to learn his face. A faint scar blends into his upper lip, round like a chicken pox scar. My thumb traces it, and Boone's lips fall apart, his thin lips pinker in the middle.

Another scar cuts through the tip of his eyebrow, deeper and fresher than the other, and I find myself wanting to know the story behind it. Wanting to know all of his stories.

"My boyfriend died."

The words are out of my mouth before I even realized I was forming them.

Boone's eyes flash open, but I don't see pity. Only confusion. He steps back, and I already miss the closeness.

"Why don't we sit down and you can talk to me about it?"

"Do you want anything to drink?" I ask, and yes, it's only to try to put more space between me and this inevitable conversation.

His gentle smile is understanding, but still he shakes his head. He leads me to my leather couch and pulls a knee up so he can face me as we sink into the full cushions. His hand is only slightly smaller than mine, but it feels bigger as he kneads my palm with his thumb.

"You don't have to tell me if you don't want to," he says. "And we don't have to do anything."

God, this man. I haven't even gotten to taste his lips and already I know I'd regret missing out.

"Dylan and I were together for nine years." I focus on the window and the way the early evening sun leaves patterns on the wall. Boone's thumb doesn't falter its rhythm. "Thirteen months ago, he had a sudden cardiac arrest. That's what they called it."

I measure my breaths to keep them even.

"Way to kill the mood, huh?" I risk a glance at Boone, whose gaze still warms everywhere it grazes. "I wanted you to know; that way if I acted weird, you would know it wasn't because of you."

Boone carefully kneels on the couch and straddles a leg over my lap. He sits far enough back that our crotches don't touch, but my cock still thickens from the proximity.

His hand cups my face this time, rough skin that tells me he's good with his hands and sends shivers up my spine at the possibilities. His eyes ask for permission. I'm a little lost in those eyes, so that I'm not sure I even manage a nod, but he reads my wishes like my face is a book. His tongue wets his lips before they meet mine, soft and wet, but a warmth that I feel everywhere. When he breathes, I think he must be inhaling pieces of me and feeding part of himself back to me through his barely parted mouth.

I open to meet him, and he still tastes of coffee and spice. His tongue strokes mine as his kisses become more demanding, so intense I'm dizzy with them. His mouth devours me, and my insides sigh like they've been waiting for this moment, like they didn't understand the beauty of kissing until now.

When we break apart, his nose rests against mine and I can feel the puffs of air against my lips and cheek as he catches his breath. Thumbs stroke my jaw and fingers caress my neck, like he doesn't want to let go.

As oxygen returns to my brain, I realize Boone still hasn't moved closer on my lap, partly because I've been clutching at his knees for dear life and partly because he's being careful with me. The straining at his zipper indicates he's willing, and I reach for his thighs to tug him closer until our clothes brush.

Boone whimpers and the muscles in his thighs flex under my palms. The sound goes straight to my dick. It's been too long, and I'm not sure I can last once we get going.

"You're so beautiful like this," I tell him, sliding my hands up and down his thighs, loving the way they tense and twitch at my touch. "But I don't want to come in my pants. Not before I get a chance to see you naked."

My fingers search for smooth skin under the edge of his thin t-shirt. It's a chilly day for April, but you wouldn't know it by the warm expanses that my hands explore. His eyes droop lower with every caress into the dip of his abs and over the soft skin covering his rock-hard pecs. My thumbs find the tight buds of his nipples and his cock jumps closer of its own accord. I can't stand it anymore; I have to see that amazing body. He whimpers when I pull my hands away, but it turns into a sigh when I lift the hem of his shirt up, and he raises his arms for me to finish the job. His hands fall back to rest gently on my shoulders and his eyes cautiously study mine as I take him in.

Silas Boone is stunning without a shirt. Greek God level. Chisel him in marble, or even just make me a plaster cast of that torso, because holy hell. Although a plaster cast would tug at those soft hairs sprinkled between his pecs that lead to a glorious trail down his pants. My mouth waters at the thought, and it's my dick jumping this time, bouncing against his groin and creating sparks of pleasure.

"Tell me a story," I say, partly because I need a way to calm down before this is over too quickly, and partly because I've been curious ever since our talk at the coffee shop. "You mentioned how hot your time with Jay was. Tell me about it."

I run a finger between his nipples as I talk, tweaking the left one when I ask him to tell me about it. His eyes darken with lust, whether from the idea of his time with Jay or because of the attention I'm giving him, and I want to see more of it.

"Was it because he topped you?" I ask and pinch his other nipple this time, eliciting a moan from his parted lips.

Boone swallows a few times before he can speak.

"He didn't actually top me."

My hand drifts to his tented jeans and I cup the bulge there with one hand, feathering the hairs above it back and forth with the thumb of my other hand.

"Then what was so hot?"

He stutters a few times, but his eyes are fully closed now and he can't focus. The poor dear. I give his ass a sharp swat and his eyes fly open, almost entirely black now.

"Up you go."

I hold out my hands to help him steady himself on his shaky

legs. He wobbles like a newborn deer, so I assist with stripping him of the rest of his clothing and ask the question again. He stands before me, completely naked, and I lean back against the couch to admire the view.

Boone's cock is cut and thick, with a delicious vein popping out in the middle. Precum beads the tip, and I'm tempted to lean forward and lick it off, but I'd rather tease him some more, since he seems to love it.

My hand moves to my shirt buttons but hesitates.

"Answer me, and I'll remove my shirt."

His sharp inhale tells me I've properly motivated him. I debate whether I'm going to have to remind him of the question again, then he wets his lips to speak.

"H-he had me naked on his bed, hands behind my head. He wouldn't let me touch him or myself."

I can see that from Jay. Just because he's small doesn't mean he isn't obviously a toppy little man. Picturing the two of them together like that? I only wish I had been there to see it in person. The thought has me so hot, it reminds me that I owe him a striptease.

I pop the first button of my shirt and drift my fingers down to the next.

"Go on."

Boone's eyes are glued to the bit of chest peeking out from my splayed shirt. His hands fidget at his sides, but he keeps talking.

"He sat over me and jacked himself."

"Touch yourself like he did," I say as I open another button, and then another when he complies with my instructions and wraps his fingers around his straining cock. I can tell by his dazed expression that he's remembering his time with Jay clearly as he's acting it out for me. My cock pulses in my pants. I need to remove them soon before I make a mess.

My shirt hangs completely open now, and I push back the sides to expose my nipples to the air. I wax my chest and groin, a habit from my time in California that I can't seem to break, so all he can see is the contrast of my bare skin with my snow-white shirt.

My fingers linger at my belt as I prod him, because his hand has stilled as his gaze zeroes in on my chest and drops to my groin. "And then?"

His hand starts stroking again, long strokes that swipe across his head each time and spread his precum along his shaft. I long to run my tongue along his length and lap it up, but I reward him instead by undoing my pants and shoving them and my briefs down to my ankles. My own cock is uncut, the head peeking out and shiny with arousal, and he moans at the sight.

"He came all over my chest and my stomach, but he didn't let me come." I can't hold back a moan of my own at the image, and it spurs him further. "I was supposed to meet up with him again. He said if I was good, he'd let me come then."

My brain tries to grasp the fact that Boone's hottest experience was a time when he didn't even get to come. I imagine Jay marking him with his cum, and I have to clamp hard around the base of my dick to keep from blowing.

I lean forward to grasp the backs of his thighs and walk him back to the couch. My face is so near his cock, I can't resist reaching out with my tongue and giving it a quick swipe. He's salty and sweet, and I have to force myself not to take him completely into my mouth. Another time. Right now, I know exactly what I want from him.

"Well, unfortunately for you, orgasm denial is not one of my kinks. I can't wait to see you come apart from my hand."

I pat my lap and lean back so he can return to straddle me, and when our cocks collide, we both groan from the pleasure that sparks between us.

Only for Us

"I'm okay with that too," he says, his voice huskier than before.

His cock has been slicked enough from his precum that we slide together when I grab us both in one hand. Boone's eyes squeeze shut and his mouth sags open, heavy breaths puffing through his lips in time with my strokes. Beautiful.

"When you fantasized about it," I say, trying to delay the inevitable that seems on the cusp of crashing down on me. "And I know just by looking at you that you did. What did you wish would have happened that next day?"

He forces his words out between breaths. "Don't you feel funny, hearing things I wish I had done with another man?"

His eyes stay closed, vulnerable, and I need to reassure him that this isn't him cheating on a boyfriend again, or even being disloyal to me in the moment. I can understand how, based on his experience, it could seem that way, but I want nothing more in this moment than to make him fly.

"Since moving to Fort Collins, Jay has come to mean a great deal to me. So, to answer your question, no. I love hearing about how a man I care about would bring pleasure to another man I care about."

"Fuck," he groans as his head drops back, exposing the length of his neck.

I lean forward and suck against his pulse point, then bite and suck my way down that sensitive skin. He bucks his hips, thrusting his cock further into my tight grasp.

"God, you're about to burst, aren't you? I bet the two of you were beautiful together."

"Yeah. Oh God," he says with a groan as he spills his seed over my hand. I hold him tight with my free arm as his body jerks his completion and guide him to rest on my chest when he slumps, spent and sated.

I release his cock, but use his cum to continue jerking

myself, replaying the look on his face, the tightening of his hands around my shoulders until I could guarantee bruises, the tensing of his abs as he came, until I come too. Streaks of white splatter my stomach before I change my aim to make sure I mark Boone too.

Now he's been marked by both Jay and me.

Somehow that feels right.

There's a niggle of an idea forming in the back of my brain. One that I can't dwell on too much right now, since I just came my brains out. But something that I can tell, once I have time to mold it into a fully formed thought, is going to change everything.

8

JAY

My knitting chair usually calms me down with its cozy throws and comfy pillows and the rhythmic clacking of needles. I can stretch out and lose myself in a project. Instead, I'm on my third screw-up of the night, having to slide the stitches off the needle and undo them, one by one. My mind had wandered and I knitted instead of purled. This baby blanket will not be screwed up on account of Cameron and Silas-fucking-Boone.

Yeah, I found out his name around the same time he used me to cheat on his boyfriend. He obviously wasn't moved to do the same, since he clearly zeroed in on my nametag at the coffee shop earlier.

I had planned to make a chicken pot pie for dinner, but I don't trust myself in a kitchen right now. I'm too keyed up and angry, and no amount of knitting is coaxing me off that resentment ledge.

Seriously. Out of all the fucking guys in the world he could have chosen. Silas-fucking-Boone.

My phone vibrates on the side table and I answer the call on speaker, shouting "Hello," so I don't have to put down my needles.

"Hey, Jay. I was wondering if you wanted to hang tonight." Kieran's voice fills the room.

"You mean Ted is willing to do without you for a whole evening?"

"He's doing a gaming party for the employees at Game Over. There are a bunch of new releases they wanted to 'test.' And I use the word very loosely."

I've never been invited, but from how Kieran has described them before, it sounds more like a bunch of grown men pretending to be teenagers at a sleepover – eating junk food, playing video games, and talking smack all night. Not exactly my kind of scene, but Kieran usually joins in.

"Why aren't you going this time?"

"Not really feeling it. I'd rather hang with you. Plus, Craig will hound me about the wedding. I agreed to be his best man, not his flower girl. I don't know anything about table decorations."

Ted owns a video game store called Game Over, and Craig, Kieran's other best friend, is the manager. Kieran got the great honor of being asked to be Craig's best man, which we all assumed meant very little. Craig's better half, Zach, is a planner – color-coordinated spreadsheets and all. We naturally assumed that Craig wouldn't have much for Kieran to do besides get him to the church, or wherever they end up having their wedding, on time, and plan the bachelor party. But Craig, wanting to make Zach's every dream come true, has been more involved in planning and thus Kieran has been tasked with some truly odd requests. Dove rentals (which thank goodness the task went to Kieran because Ted gave him a boatload of articles about why they are a terrible and cruel idea) got nixed immediately, but Kieran's been tagged to find out about flash mobs (please God, say that group of gaming nerds are planning on dancing for Zach because that is something I want to see) and how to brew a craft beer specially for the wedding. It sounds like he has even more unusual requests to fulfill.

"Sure. Grab dinner, so I don't have to cook."

"Aww, I was going to see if you would be willing to show me how to make those vegan Linzer cookies you do."

"Hang on."

I carefully roll up my needles in the blanket to make sure no stitches will slip off and tuck it away in the basket next to my chair. Taking the phone with me, I investigate my cupboards.

"Bring some of Ted's jam. It's the one thing I don't have."

"You're the best."

"I know. See you in a bit."

A half hour later, I've got the kitchen cleaned up, the chicken pot pie ingredients stowed, and the Linzer cookie ingredients out and ready. Kieran knocks as he enters, a habit that I had to drill into him was perfectly acceptable. I never have men over, since I usually have to venture out of town for my hookups.

He tosses a pizza box onto my clean countertop, earning him a scowl, but carefully hands me the jar of Ted's homemade strawberry rhubarb preserves.

I pull out a slice covered in cheese and BBQ chicken and pineapple, because Kieran is my pizza soulmate, and fold it in half before biting off the pointy end.

Kieran's eyebrows lift until his forehead is a mash of freckles. "Hungry?"

"Famished," I say with a huge sigh. Food will make me feel better. "I was too upset to eat, but now I think food is just what I need to fuel my rage and pick me back up."

"Uh-oh. What has you so upset? Did Troye Sivan change his hair color again?"

"Honey, you know his going blond was a travesty. People

thought I was copying *him*. If he doesn't change it back soon, I'm going to have to rethink my look, and then all the time and effort to keep this platinum blond will have been for nothing."

"You could always go back to grey."

I stab my crust toward him. "Don't make me cut a bitch. Plus, you're awfully cocky for a guy hoping I'll teach him to make cookies for his boyfriend."

Kieran throws up his hands in surrender before returning to his pizza, which he eats at normal human speed while I reach for my second slice.

"So, what's the matter?"

Damn.

"You ever have one of those days where you feel like everything's against you?"

He quirks an eyebrow as if questioning whether or not I remember everything going on with him when we first met – his sleaze of a boss hitting on him and not taking rejection well.

"Right. Well, this is just one of those days."

"I'm going to need a little more than that," he says, finally reaching for another slice so I feel like less of a pig.

My hand hovers over the box, but I withdraw and turn around to wash my hands instead. Can't have greasy fingers while baking cookies.

"I don't know if you noticed or not, but Cameron and I kind of flirt with each other."

He waits to speak until I turn back around and see that his look is as dry as his voice. "You don't say."

"I never expected anything to happen. Even if he weren't still getting over the loss of his partner, I'm sure we wouldn't exactly mesh in the bedroom."

Kieran shrugs and pops a fallen piece of pineapple into his mouth. "Eh. You might be surprised what those big guys like in the bedroom."

When I don't pick up my jaw from the floor fast enough, Kieran claps with glee. "Yes! I finally shocked you. I didn't think it was possible."

"We are definitely coming back around to that. In fact, screw my problems. I want to hear all about the things Ted likes that would surprise me. Go on," I say and lean my chin against my palm, gazing at Kieran. "Linzer cookies can wait."

"Nope." Kieran washes his own hands and returns to the table, finding the recipe and looking it over. "Linzer cookies can begin, along with the story of what Cameron did to upset you. And don't pretend like you can't multitask. I've seen you at work."

"Fine." I reach into the cabinets below our feet and pull out the needed bowls and measuring cups, and Kieran gets started with measuring out the ingredients. He's all elbows and shoulders, so I move to the side while he works.

"Cameron brought his date in to Espresso Patronum earlier, which already, I was like, really? Did he not get that he was rubbing my face in it?"

"Oh, man. I'm sorry." Kieran extends a hand to pat my shoulder, but I shove a whisk into it before it reaches me. I don't want to be pitied. I want to be angry, dammit.

"It gets worse. It was a guy I had hooked up with, once upon a time. A guy I thought finally saw and wanted the real me."

Kieran knew I had trouble finding guys who wanted me to top them, so his look only gets more pitying. I grab the bowl and the whisk from him and spend the next few minutes sharing the rest of the tale of Silas-fucking-Boone while taking my aggression out on flour, sugar, and coconut oil. Most days I regret not having an electric mixer, but not today.

"Wow." It's Kieran's turn to pick up his jaw when I finish telling the G-rated version of the story. "Does Cameron know?"

"Obviously not. He introduced us to each other just as sweet and innocent as could be. His eyes fucking sparkled, like he was so happy and proud of his date. I can't ruin that for him, even if I am pissed he didn't pick me."

With the dough ready to be rolled out, I show Kieran how I use more coconut oil on two parchment sheets instead of flouring a surface, because it would add too much flour to the mixture, and vegan cookies are always at risk of being too dry.

It preoccupies him enough for me to sit back and reflect. I'm not mad at Cameron. I'm not really even mad at Boone. It's more that I'm disappointed that I will never be anyone's first choice. I'll always be the guy on the side or the guy at the club. But any time I've actually tried to date someone, they just don't take me seriously. What is it about me that screams I'm good enough to fuck but not good enough to meet the parents?

Ugh, this really has turned into a pity party, and I am so over it.

"Okay, enough about me," I say as I pass over the cookie cutters and set him to work. "How can I help with Craig's floral arrangements?"

"Oh God," Kieran groans. "Don't remind me. Zach wanted to save money and do it himself, so he's trying to learn how to make boutonnieres and Craig volunteered to do the centerpieces. Which really means he volunteered me to do the centerpieces. At least the ceremony is going to be outside in the gazebo of the Armstrong House, so it isn't like they'll need flowers there."

I clutch at my chest but refrain from saying, "Of course they'll still need flowers around the gazebo." This isn't my wedding. But I can help with the centerpieces since they, by way of Kieran – sort of – asked.

"What does your next Saturday morning look like?"

Kieran smirks and I give him a hip check, the first all night that was intended. Seriously, I've seen him in the kitchen with

Only for Us

Ted before and they practically move together as one unit. Who knew we'd have so much difficulty not poking each other's eyes out working side by side?

"Okay, after you and your man make wild monkey love that I apparently would be surprised by and want to hear all about, we can go thrifting. I have a cute idea that wouldn't cost them a lot of money but would go great with the antique feel of the Armstrong House."

Kieran clasps my head in both hands and lands a loud smack on my forehead.

"Bless you."

I run a hand down my side. "Obviously, already done."

Kieran laughs, and we return our attention to making sickeningly cute love gifts for his man.

After Kieran leaves, I take a bite of one of the few cookies he left for me and make a decision. The cookie melts in your mouth with subtle flavor, which blends perfectly with the sharpness of the jam. I really can bake, and if I have nothing else in my life to do but craft and bake for others, I might as well pursue it. Tomorrow evening, I'm going to bake more muffins, perfecting the recipes I put together the other day, and present them to Larry on Friday.

It's time I take that next step.

My chest begins to puff up with confidence, and I set about making a list of things I'll need for my next baking night, including a bottle of wine. It will kind of be like a date with my muffins. No, that sounds wrong.

I laugh at myself, finally cheering up after my shitshow of a day, when my phone vibrates on the counter.

Cameron: Can we get together tomorrow night and talk?

And just like that, my good mood pops faster than a balloon at a *Hellraiser* convention.

9

CAMERON

I think I first fall in love with Jay upon entering his home. Charming doesn't cover it. I'd say it's more like the man is bursting with love to give and had no other outlet for it, so he spent it on his home instead of another man.

It's also a much-needed reminder that Jay isn't Dylan. If I were a psychologist and not a lawyer, I'd probably wonder why I keep conflating the two and why it's so important to me that I prove myself wrong.

After dropping Boone back off at his car last night, I sent a text to Kieran asking for Jay's number. The request earned me a surprising "Really?" text followed by a bunch of expressionless-faced emojis that I didn't really get. Still, he gave me the number, and I immediately texted Jay, asking if we could get together to talk. When he said he had lots of baking to do, I offered to go to him. Now, walking through the front door into a wall of cinnamon and apple, I can only hope he needs a taste tester.

"The cavalry has arrived," I say and rub my hands together eagerly. "What do you need me to eat? I mean do."

I eye the stack of muffins sitting off to the side, the lovely aroma coming from them calling me forward for a bite.

Jay waves a metal contraption in my direction, blocking my entrance to the kitchen. "I need you to stay on that side of the counter. I bake alone."

"Sounds lonely."

"Sounds safe."

He sets the metal thing in a bowl, then disappears into his pantry, returning a minute later with his arms loaded down. A small jar almost escapes, and I rush over to catch it.

"Uh-uh," Jay says as he lets his armful tumble onto the counter and goes about setting everything upright. "This is my space. That is your space. The two shall not cross."

"I just saved your space from being covered in," I read the jar still in my hand, "nutmeg. You're welcome."

Jay plucks the nutmeg from my hand with a curt, "Thank you."

"What's that metal thing?" I ask with a nod to the bowl.

"See? This is why you stay on your side. If you don't even know what a sifter is, I'd really have my hands full."

"Yes, I've heard I'm definitely two handfuls, not just one," I say with a wink that earns me a tut.

Jay begins to measure flour into the sifter.

"I doubt your boyfriend would appreciate you flirting with me."

Ah, is that a green-eyed monster I see peeking out of Jay? It gives me hope for the reason that I came here, and I'll admit, it's flattering. I wasn't one hundred percent sure that Jay's flirting hadn't just been Jay versus a sign that he was interested. Now I'm betting on the latter.

"Actually, I know he would. He'd just be disappointed he couldn't be here to flirt with you too."

Jay's movements falter and he stares at me with question marks in his eyes. When he shakes his head and returns his focus to his baking, his shoulders slump.

Only for Us

"Crap, what number was that?"

"Three," I guess.

"Are you sure? I'm going to present these muffins to Larry tomorrow and ask to do the baking for the shop. They have to be perfect."

The vulnerability in his voice makes my chest ache.

"Then in that case, I'd start over. I wasn't paying attention either."

Jay gives me a cross look as he empties the bowl, like I'd dare to mess with him, but really, he should know that I would love to mess with him by now. I hold up my hands in surrender and wander around to look at the rest of his place. The kitchen opens into the living room, so he can watch as I walk around and view the artwork and run my hand along the crocheted blankets. There's a bag full of soft-looking yarn that I kneel to touch but get a sharp warning.

"Careful. It's a blanket I'm working on for my soon-to-be niece or nephew. If it slips off the needles, I will hurt you. And not in the fun way."

I chuckle, but back away slowly from the knitting.

"What's all this?" I ask, waving over the dozens of magazines laid out on his creatively decorated coffee table. Sticky notes and tabs pepper the pages filled with different flowers.

Jay counts out loud as he empties the final cup of flour into the sifter, then finally deigns to pay attention to me.

"Kieran was tasked with coming up with centerpiece ideas for Craig and Zach's wedding. I offered to help."

His eyes pierce me and I feel a lump form in my throat. It isn't just that he's gorgeous, although he is – willowy and pale, with eyes a swirling blue-green of intensity, and a strength that gives his body grace, even when he lacks confidence. No, it's the way he cares for his friends and the ones he loves. It makes me long to be a part of that inner circle.

"You know, I never did get Kieran and Ted a moving-in-together present. Have any great ideas?"

"You lived with Ted for a month when you first moved here. And you work with Kieran. You'd probably know just as well as I."

Yes, but I don't have his obvious creativity. He'd no doubt wave it off like he does most compliments, but it's true.

I stay silent, running my hand along the lacquered top of the coffee table where it's visible, appreciating the photos that he's put beneath them. He's so talented and he doesn't even know it.

"Well, there's a place in town that does vegan cooking lessons. They might have fun with that. Or get them a stack of board games, although trust me, you don't want to know what they do with them."

Jay pretends to shudder, which only serves to pique my interest. Maybe I'll taunt Kieran with that info at work and see what happens.

"You make gifts, bake, and help decorate weddings. Are you the next Martha Stewart?"

"You jest, but that woman has a million-dollar empire that even prison couldn't crumble. I should be so lucky. Except without the jail part." Jay paused for second and added, "And not so damn stuffy."

"I wasn't joking. I think you're amazing."

Jay fumbles a measuring spoon and it skitters across the table.

"You know, it's taking me twice as long to bake with you here," he says, giving me a frown that his eyes contradict.

"If you'd let me help ..."

He sighs and scoots a muffin tin across the counter and plops a plastic container of liners on top.

"Here. Stay quiet for five minutes and line the muffin tin for me."

I flash him my toothiest grin and say, "See? I knew you couldn't resist me."

Jay shakes his head. "Not listening," he sing-songs.

I quietly take orders as he finishes. I want him to know I don't mind his bossiness, but I also simply enjoy watching him work. I never knew things like stirring batter could be so sensual, but Jay doesn't just beat the ingredients together. His arm moves with steady but gentle swoops and turns, more like a dance than baking. His eyes focus on the bowl, clearly watching for the right moment when it all comes together and he suddenly stops and sets the bowl down.

A tendril of hair flops from behind his ears and he tries to blow it back. When that doesn't work, I risk crossing the line into the kitchen and tuck it behind a slightly pointy ear. If my finger lingers over the soft, velvety shell as I set his hair right, well, Jay freezes and pretends not to notice. I, however, will file away for the future how delicate and sensitive his ears are.

"So, uh, you wanted to talk to me about something?"

His attention is on making perfect scoops of batter into the muffin tin, but I can see the tips of his ears, the ones that I'm going to have fantasies about in the future, turn pink.

"Yes, but I'll wait until those are in the oven. I wouldn't want to break your concentration."

"Oh good," he says, his hands slowing as he finishes filling the tin. "That's not worrisome at all."

Jay turns his back to me as he puts the tin in the oven, then returns to the counter, cleaning to keep his hands busy.

"I was talking with Boone yesterday," I say. Jay's head pops up with a frown, like I guessed he would. "He told me about his past, about how he cheated on his boyfriend with you." His mouth opens to protest, and I add, "He made it clear you had no idea. He only blames himself."

Jay sighs and returns his attention to the counter. His frown remains in place as he scrubs at patches of flour with a sponge.

"And why are you telling me this? If you came to apologize on his behalf, don't bother."

"He clearly still has feelings for you. He told me all about your time together."

"Right," Jay scoffs.

There it is. The reaction I was waiting for. He's angry, but mostly to cover his hurt. It's that reaction that gives me hope for my ploy to work.

"I was wondering if you might still have feelings for him? If you felt that your time together was as special as he obviously does?"

Jay's forehead wrinkles and he studies me for a bit before finally speaking.

"I'm confused. Are you trying to set me up with the guy you're dating?"

"No," I say as calmly and dispassionately as I would presenting a case in court. I need him to know I'm serious, and not just jerking him around. "I'm trying to determine if you would be open to dating us both."

"I'm still not following," he says with a shake of his head.

I come around the counter, crossing the line-that-shall-not-be-crossed, and take his hand. He lets me lead him to his couch, and I sit facing him with his hand still in mine.

"I really like you. I've enjoyed flirting with you, but more than that, I think you're pretty damn special. I was scared of getting close to anyone again so soon after Dylan, but I'd like to get to know you better."

"And Boone?"

"I also like Boone. It has happened faster than I was expecting, but I have already developed feelings for him too. I care for him, want to protect him and be there for him."

Jay takes a shuddering breath but doesn't say anything. His expression is closed off, not giving anything away.

"At first, I was thinking that I would have to choose. That is, if you were interested in going out with me, too." My voice wavers for the first time, and I take a steadying breath. His silence is unnerving. Worse than any judge I've ever appeared before. "But after I saw you and Boone together, and heard him speak about your time together with such passion and longing, I thought there might be another option."

When he still doesn't respond, I add, "I'd like for us to try dating. Together. The three of us."

"A throuple," he says without inflection, and I curse myself that I've totally misread him. I expected doubt or maybe even amusement at the idea of three people in a relationship, but not anger.

"I hate that term," I say with a forced laugh. I internally debate running away, bolting for the door and texting him tomorrow that it was all a joke. Ha ha. I'm suddenly hot all over at the horrible decision I've made in coming here and proposing this harebrained idea.

Just when my legs tense, about to put the whole running idea into practice, Jay barks out a genuine laugh.

"Me too. I think triad is even worse. It sounds like some secret organization, not a relationship."

I offer a hesitant smile, but it fades quickly as I wait for him to say more. He picks at his ripped jeans, the loosest things I've ever seen on Jay's lower half, but still fitting with his style, and I wait. He coughs and shifts on the couch, and I continue to wait.

"It's not that I'm not interested," he finally says, and I release the breath I didn't realize I was holding. "Let's call it hesitant."

"Because of Boone?"

"Well, that's a large part of it. He cheated on someone. Used me. I don't trust him, and I don't think that's a great way to begin any kind of relationship, but especially one as complicated as what you're proposing."

I nod my understanding.

"It's not my place to convince you of Boone's sincerity or regret. That's why I'm hoping you'd agree to go out on a date with us. We can talk more then, and you can determine whether you think you could forgive him and trust him. Do you trust me?"

Jay rolls his eyes and relaxes back into his sofa.

"Of course I trust you."

"Well, then trust that I think this could work. I think if you hear him out, you will be inclined to forgive Boone. And trust that I think the three of us together would be amazing, not just sexually – although I'm confident that would be explosive – but emotionally as well."

Jay narrows his eyes but turns his body on the couch, pulling his knees up and propping his head on an elbow. He's still relaxed. The initial anger has burned off, and surprise has given way to interest, but skepticism is not so easily dismissed.

"Why are you pushing this? You've been mourning Dylan and hesitant to move on. Which I understand. I do. But it makes this even more confusing. I'd have thought you'd be running from this idea, not cheering us into it."

He's not wrong. I've thought about that very question all night long. I've been so nervous to ask Jay out, worried it would feel like a repeat of my relationship with Dylan, worried I would just be seeking out a second-best placeholder for the thing I can no longer have. It wouldn't have been fair to anyone, so I stayed away.

Then I thought, maybe I didn't deserve Jay, or Boone. I've had my love. It seems selfish to ask for more, and not just one more, but two at that. But then I remembered something my mom said when she got remarried. I was eight, and angry that she could so easily replace the love she had for my dad with love for another man.

"Baby, love isn't like that," she said, though at the time I didn't believe her. "Love isn't finite. You don't have a limited amount that you have to take away from one person in order to give it to another. Love is infinite. The more people you have to care for, the more love you have to give."

It didn't take long for Celeste and me to realize that her words were true, at least when it came to her love for us. Granted, I'm not sure how Mom would react to me taking her advice to justify starting a relationship with two men.

"Maybe that's why. I know what it's like to have lost someone that I loved. I feel like sitting at home in sadness would not honor his memory. And believe me, if you had met Dylan, you'd understand that he'd be cheering this on harder than anyone else. Yes, I'm scared of getting hurt again. So scared. But what if it's worth it?"

Jay's eyes grow misty the way they always do when I talk about Dylan. It makes me wonder if he ever lost someone too, the way he reacts. He takes a deep breath, as if preparing to speak, but his eyes widen and he turns to the kitchen in a panic.

"Fuck, I forgot the timer."

He checks on the muffins and I once again cross the line that I'm not supposed to. I touch his shoulder, feeling bone and tendon and muscle react to my fingers. It sends a thrill up my hand, realizing this is the first time I've touched Jay in this way. A way I've wanted for so long, if I'm being honest with myself.

"Are you okay?"

"It's just so fucking unfair, what you had to go through. You're so strong, and so good. Things like that shouldn't happen to guys like you."

"You hurt for me?"

His eyes mist over again and he looks back to the oven,

busying himself with lights and oven mitts. Anything to avoid my gaze.

"Oh, my sweet Jaybird," I whisper. "I'm a fool."

His shoulders shake under my hand, and I pull him to me. He buries himself in my chest, shaking from the effort of not crying.

"Aren't we all?" he says, his voice muffled by the cotton of my shirt, but still sounding slightly on the edge of panicked.

"Yes, but hopefully we're starting to figure things out. It shouldn't have taken so long."

"I'll think about it," he says quietly into my shirt pocket as he rubs his face back and forth against the soft fabric. I'm not sure he realizes he's doing it. It seems to be one of those comfort things that people do subconsciously. "The date. The three of us. I'll think about it."

"That's all I can ask," I respond, but my hands continue to soothe him and hold him tight. I won't pressure any more, but that doesn't mean I won't try to persuade in other ways.

What started as a tentative idea is now cemented in my mind as the only right course of action, and I'm not one for giving up.

10

JAY

The last person I expect to interrupt the mid-morning lag stares at me sheepishly from behind hazel eyes.

"Can I help you?"

It comes out angry and sharp, with none of my usual flirtiness. I'm mostly a flirt because I enjoy it. It feels good to exude the sensuality that I feel inside, and make others feel good as a result of sharing it. But when I work, a lot of it comes down to tips. I really don't know where my natural flirt begins and ends any longer, it has taken over my personality in such a fundamental way.

With Boone staring across the counter at me, however, every bit of flirt shrinks away and hides.

"I was hoping we could talk?" he says more than asks and jams his hands into his jacket pockets. "I would have texted, but I don't have your number."

Usually about this time of morning, I'd be grabbing a coffee myself and taking it back to the kitchen to rest before the lunch rush. Anna is behind the counter, restocking the milks, and Larry's already taken off for the day. He's the least involved owner I've ever met. Comes in for a few hours, enough to distract us during the morning rush, then always claims business elsewhere. Once in a while, he'll be back in the evenings to check in on things or bring by new glassware or décor or equipment. But most days, he stays away.

Of course, that means I won't hear his opinion on my muffins until tomorrow morning, and my stomach is tied in knots over it. I had hoped for something a little more interested or supportive than, "I'll take 'em home to Wendy and see what she thinks," but apparently that's all I'm getting. I can only hope Wendy, his wife, likes them enough to recommend me for the job.

"Go take your break with pretty boy," Anna whispers behind my back and I flinch.

"Never mind," Boone says, mistaking my flinch for something else. "We can talk another time. Sorry for bothering you."

"No." I fling out a hand to stop him and he freezes. "Let me refresh my coffee. Do you want anything?"

"Just a plain coffee is fine for me too."

With my hands full with two mugs, one of which I added a little milk to, remembering how Boone took it before, I wander between the tables to put as much space between us and Anna as possible. Boone follows behind and pulls out a chair for me when I stop at the table in the corner.

"I'm guessing Cameron told you his idea?" I ask as I sit. I don't have much break time, so there's no point in beating around the bush.

Boone pulls out the chair across from me, and I pretend not to notice the way his muscles flex under his shirt as he shrugs off his jacket and hangs it on the back of his chair. His shyness has given way to purpose, and he plants his palms on the table in front of him.

"Yeah. And before it goes any further, if it is going to go any further, I need to talk to you."

I gesture to the two shaking mugs between us, like the table is his. "Shoot."

"I'm sure you must hate me after everything that happened. I tried to tell Cameron that I'd already screwed up, and there's no coming back from that. He had some pretty words about forgiveness and everyone making mistakes, but some mistakes are too big."

He's right. I've held in that anger for years now. Angry that he made me an accomplice in his cheating. Angry that he wasn't mine to take. But most of all, angry that everything I told myself about who I was and what I wanted wasn't a lie. There had been a strong, beautiful man eager to give me everything I wanted, and it had given me hope. To have that torn away in an instant, and never to be able to replicate it again, well, that had been the cruelest part of all.

"I want you to know how sorry I am," he says when I stay quiet, my brain full of thoughts and emotions that I thought had been long buried. "I wouldn't blame you if you didn't want to have anything to do with me. But Cameron ..."

He takes a sip of his coffee, wincing at the heat. It seems to give him the jolt he needs to continue.

"Cameron is special, and I know he wants you. If you don't think you can do it, be with me too, then I'll bow out. I don't want my mistakes to ruin things for the two of you."

His eyes droop with sadness, like having to give up Cameron – or even me – is the hardest thing he's ever done, but there he sits, the handsome martyr, drinking too-hot coffee with slumped shoulders like he deserves it.

When Cameron brought up the idea, my first thought was that I was coming in second place, a third wheel tacked on at the end as an afterthought. As horrible as it may sound, the fact that Boone seems to think of himself as the third wheel makes me feel a little better about the whole thing. Like maybe all of us could be coupled up in different ways, but the point is, we don't want to be that way.

"Why?"

He nods, working through answers in his head. "I'd never cheated on anyone before, but it scared me. I don't want to be that kind of person. I don't deserve to come between you two."

My brain works through his sentence, trying to figure out what he means, when I realize he's answering why he would agree to step aside for me to be with Cameron. It isn't that I don't disagree. I'm still angry with him, but I doubt anything that I've lost or felt could compare with the self-flagellation this man has obviously put himself through. Maybe, like before, he needs me to punish him. Make everything okay.

"No, I meant why did you cheat in the first place?"

The side of his mouth twitches in an almost-smile before he schools it back. "It's funny. Between my dad and my coaches, you'd think I'd be used to taking orders. But their yelling, their orders, the purpose was always to rile me up, motivate me to do better, work harder, be more. The way you said things, ordering me, talking about punishing me, it didn't get me going, it relaxed me. Lit me up inside, like I could just let go, and that would be enough."

He takes a sip of coffee and continues. "It was wrong to forget about Arthur. He had called earlier that day, after my dad had railed at me for my injury and not working through it, but being with him was also work. It wasn't fair to cheat on him; I should have realized sooner how I felt, but being with him felt like work too."

"Have you ever apologized to Arthur?" I ask. He seems to need the forgiveness more than I need to hold on to my anger or resentment. Maybe it would be good for him, if he hasn't already.

"No. He wouldn't speak to me after that, not that I could

blame him. I just had my own issues, and I couldn't find my way around them to ever be comfortable with him. It wasn't his fault, but he was so smart and so motivated, it made me feel inferior by comparison. I always had a dumb jock complex. It's no excuse for what I did, but it's why. I lumped him and my dad and my coaches and football and all of that together that day, and just wanted a break from it all."

I could see that. He's right, it didn't excuse his cheating, but it did make sense.

"And then I came along and gave you a way to let it all out."

Boone's eyes look past me, like he's remembering that day, and I shift in my seat at the sight of his flushed skin.

"I forgot about everything else, and I just wanted to be with you. Not using you as an excuse, because I still have a brain and a mouth. I should have used them. But what you gave me back then, it was like a piece of me I never even knew was missing had suddenly been found. Nothing's been the same since." His eyes flash at mine. "Fuck, when you said the word 'punished.' My whole life changed."

God, thinking about all the ways I could punish him now, I take a sip of my drink to try and focus. Too many ideas, each one painting more erotic pictures than the last. And when you add the image of Cameron in to the mix, it's enough to make my jeans much tighter than before.

"Jay."

Anna's voice from behind the counter stirs my brain from its dirty daydreams and I realize a line has formed during our discussion.

I clear my throat and take another gulp of coffee, hoping the burn will ease my suffering before I have to stand, but the coffee has had enough time to cool. Well, if you've got it, flaunt it. Right?

"I have to get back to work."

"Of course. That's all I wanted to say anyway. Just, I'm sorry, and let me know what you decide. If it's for me to get lost, I understand."

The last of my anger dissipates as Boone bites his lip, looking so defeated. No one deserves to feel that down on themselves, and it firms my resolve toward the situation.

"We'll talk again soon," I say, and shoot him a wink that startles the mug from his hand. I flash out a hand to steady it, stroking a thumb against his slippery fingers before taking the cup from his grasp. With both of our cups in hand, I head to the counter, swishing my hips as I walk.

If Cameron wants the three of us to try something, I'm game. Whatever my previous feelings had been toward Boone, this afternoon was enough to return my confidence and bring out the toppy instincts that he seems to naturally evoke. Even if nothing more than a night comes of it, at least I'll have that.

11

BOONE

Cameron shows up to my doorstep for the date in jeans and a t-shirt – the first time I've ever seen him dressed down. I had debated dressing up, but thank goodness I stayed with my nice jeans and a button-down or I'd feel even more self-conscious right now. I pull the door shut behind me before he can peek in.

The passenger side door swings open and Jay steps out, his platinum-blond hair pulled up into a bun on the top of his head. His sheer shirt leaves little to the imagination with lots of creamy skin on display as he surges toward me and presses a kiss to my cheek. I blink in surprise. Has he forgiven me?

"Unfortunately, Cam's car doesn't have bench seats, so I'll let you have the front."

Jay climbs into the back and immediately leans forward, poking his head between the two seats and reaching for the radio. Cam bats his hand away as we get seated and seatbelts fastened.

"What did I tell you about the radio?"

"I think it's incredibly unfair for the driver to be the DJ, since

I don't have a car. And your musical taste is almost enough to have me rethinking this whole evening."

I swivel in my seat to see if Jay's joking, and he scrunches up his face at me.

"Country," he says like it's the most painful word ever. "He likes country."

"I like country," I say and see Cameron break into a grin across from me. Jay moans dramatically and flops back against the back seat.

"I'm doomed."

"So, where are we headed?"

"It's a surprise. I thought a fancy restaurant might be a little much when we're just getting to know each other," Cam says, pulling back out into traffic. I know he means a little much for me, considering I'm still getting used to being out in public. I appreciate it. Jay might have been ready for the full wining and dining experience, but the thought of a date with Cameron, much less both of them, in a romantic setting has me breaking out into a cold sweat.

When Cameron pulls his car into a parking lot, Jay leans forward again.

"Bowling? Do these look like bowling pants to you?"

"They look like I'm going to thoroughly enjoy you bending over to bowl, so yes." Cameron winks as he says it and Jay's jaw drops open.

Jay pouts as we exit the car. "You could have given a girl some notice. I wore my best clubbing clothes." He seems flummoxed when he opens the door, so I extend a hand to help him out.

"I think you look incredible," I say, my eyes drifting down of their own accord. It earns me another kiss on the cheek.

"Don't be too good," Jay whispers into my ear, "Or I won't have a reason to punish you later."

Jay continues his fake pouting inside. I love that he can be so forceful with me and yet so bratty with Cameron. It's like we bring out two different sides to his personality, so he gets more by being with the two of us together than he would with just one. I kind of feel that way myself. When Jay orders me around or threatens to punish me, it makes a certain part inside me sing out for joy, and then Cameron calms every part of me with his gentle care. I'm attracted to them both for completely different reasons, but I'd never be able to choose if I had to.

"Do you know how gross and germy bowling balls are?" Jay says, making a face as he holds the balls in both hands, testing their weights to decide which one to pick. I wait to see if his comment derails the whole evening, remembering Cameron's comment about germy pool balls. Instead, Cameron reaches into his pocket and triumphantly holds up hand sanitizer.

"I came prepared. Or you could always just roll it underhanded like that kid," Cameron jokes with a nod at a small child a few lanes away with bumper guards up.

"Aww, I thought that was lube in your pocket. Now I'm disappointed," Jay says but holds out his hands and lets Cameron squirt some hand sanitizer on them. "And don't think I won't do a granny roll, just to make you sorry for teasing me."

"I don't think anything could make Cameron sorry for teasing you," I say, and Jay flounces forward after tugging on his bowling shoes. He stands in front of the chairs where Cameron and I sit side by side, still struggling with our own shoes. He cocks a hip and one forefinger runs down Cameron's cheek and the other down mine, a trail of heat left in its wake.

"Don't you know that's just going to make me work harder?"

I know other guys might be put off by Jay's flamboyance, but I love it when he gets all flirty. It makes him seem so commanding and in control. And super hot.

I let Cameron go first so I can get my dick under control and not embarrass myself. He handles the ball like a pro, and I smirk about that to myself but don't say it out loud. Jay doesn't need any more ammo. He gets a strike on the first shot and turns back to us, treating us with an adorable victory dance.

Jay might be onto something. Maybe we should go clubbing next time.

"Now I see why you wanted to go bowling. You just wanted to show off," Jay says. "Well, two can play at that."

Jay picks up his ball and sashays toward the lane, when a booming voice from behind startles me.

"Boone?"

I turn to find a middle-aged man, wearing jeans and a CSU t-shirt while sporting a bald spot and looking for all the world like he's clinging to his college days.

"Silas Boone, man, it's an honor to meet you." It's becoming rarer and rarer these days, but I still get recognized. "It's a shame about your knee. I'm telling you, in that game against San Diego State, when you threw five hundred yards without an interception. You were untouchable. I thought for sure you'd make pro."

He takes in our little party, giving Cameron a manly nod, but recoils when his eyes get to Jay, who looks luscious bending over and rolling the ball between his legs down the lane.

"What's with the fairy?"

I freeze up, having been on the other side of this before. Not handing out the slurs, but I've been in groups that did and kept to myself instead of defending the person. Anything to keep my dad from guessing about me.

Cameron steps forward. "My boyfriend is an inexperienced bowler, but I find it rather endearing."

"Gutter ball, again, and you guys missed it," Jay says, joining the group. "I should have celebrated like I got a strike and you'd never know the difference." He leans forward and lays a hand on the stranger's arm in an exaggerated flirt. "And I'm no ordinary fairy. I'm goddamn Tinker Bell, and you know how pissy she can be, so you better get it right."

Jay winks at the man, fucking winks, then turns back to where his bowling ball has popped up.

"Oh goodie, I get another turn, right?"

"Yes, dear." I somehow find my voice, and feel a little satisfaction at the trio of surprised faces around me. "And I promise we'll be watching this time."

"Good," Jay says, the first to recover. "I'm not bending over for just anyone, you know."

"It's always nice meeting a fan," I say, extending a hand to the man who remains too startled to do anything but shake it.

I return my attention to Jay, who true to his word is bending over with the ball, looking over his shoulder to make sure he has our attention. By the time his turn is over and I look back around, my "fan" is nowhere to be seen.

"I wasn't sure how you wanted to handle that," Cameron says, clasping my shoulder from the cracked plastic chair next to me. "But I'm proud of you."

"I'd be prouder of myself if I'd done that years ago."

"Everyone has their own journey," Jay says, slouching into the seat on my other side. "We'd be a couple of assholes not to realize that."

The game continues, and although Jay and Cameron continue their teasing, they seem to have formed a common goal of covering me with support, love, protection, whatever it might be. I feel the change in their level of caring for me, and I know that this thing between us is right.

~

"We could head back to my place, for dessert," Cameron says as we change into our regular shoes. We had snacks while bowling, but it was enough to fill me up. "I promise, just more time to get to know each other. Or we could go somewhere for coffee?"

"I get enough of coffee houses during the day," Jay says. "I vote for your place. Boone?"

I nod in agreement. I've been eager for this part, although I've tried not to let on. Sex with each of them has been incredible, and I feel like the luckiest guy on Earth that I'm getting the chance at this.

At the car, I usher Jay into the passenger side and have to swallow down my arousal when he coos, "What a gentleman," at me in that tempting voice. Everything about the man is tempting, from his sheer shirt with teasing pockets over his chest, hiding just his nipples from sight, to his swaying hips and sly smile. He really is Tinker Bell, a saucy fairy sent to hypnotize me and bind me to him.

"Speaking of coffee houses," Cameron says, as he gets settled and starts the car. "What happened with Larry and your muffins? Although I hate the idea of another man sampling your muffins – unless, of course, it's Boone." He flashes wolfish teeth in the rearview mirror at me.

"Then you don't have to worry. Larry passed them off to his wife to try. I'm hoping to hear on Monday how she liked them. She's pretty picky. Whenever she comes into the coffee house with new décor, she always has a negative thing to say about any changes made. It's like Larry has one idea in mind – a nerdy place for book and coffee lovers – and she wants something more sophisticated."

"Well, the muffins I tried were not only the best-tasting ones I've ever had, but you made them so pretty, too. There's no way she won't be impressed." A tiny thread of disappointment winds itself around my chest, until Cameron adds, "You need to bake a batch for Boone. Then you'll have two men extolling the virtues of your muffins. We'll convince Larry's wife on your behalf."

Only for Us

I shouldn't feel jealous. Cameron and Jay have obviously been good friends for a while now. I just need to remember that so I don't feel like a third wheel, sitting back here alone. Jay's right. Cameron does need a vehicle with bench seats.

When we get to Cameron's apartment, I kick off my shoes by the front door. It's become habit. His apartment is so pristine, I can't help but worry about ruining it somehow.

"No worries," Cameron says, and I'm not sure if he's reading my mind or talking about something else. "No pressure. Nothing sexual. Just getting to know one another better."

I knew about Cameron's no-pressure plan from his texts earlier this week, so I prepared and plugged myself specifically with that in mind – thinking it would increase the pleasure when I had to handle myself after an evening with these sexy men. It had been torture during bowling, with all the bending over, but now it's an even worse torture, wishing I wasn't going to have to take care of myself all alone. Not that I'm not enjoying getting to know both of them, but I don't know how long I can hold out, not being able to touch either one of them.

12

JAY

"No. I appreciate the thought, but if we're going to be together, the three of us, then it's important to go ahead and find out if we're compatible in all ways. It's hard enough to find someone I mesh with sexually, but the odds that all three of us work together ..."

Boone ducks his head, studying his hands like he's never seen them before.

"Boone? Do you disagree?"

His eyes are wide as saucers at being called out, but if the three of us are going to try to do this, we need to communicate, no matter how hard or uncomfortable it may be. Cameron's fond smile that shifts back and forth between us lets me know he's on the same page.

"No. Well, yes. Not about holding off. I'm good with progressing however far you guys are willing. But I have no concerns about the sex part. I already know how incredible it is with you. And with Cameron. I think the only question left is how you two work together."

The first flash of jealousy at hearing he and Cameron have had sex morphs into a sudden jealousy at not being able to have witnessed it. I glance over Boone's shoulder to see lust rolling off Cameron in waves.

"Shall we show him how we work together?" I ask Cameron, who responds with a rumbling, "Hell, yes."

I stand and grab Boone's hands, pulling him up to face me. Cameron fits behind him, his hands clasped at Boone's hips. I cup a hand on each of their cheeks, looking first into Boone's hazel eyes, already hazy with lust. My gaze travels to Cameron, whose dark eyes are blown darker, settling the nerves in my belly and spurring me to act. As I lean over Boone's shoulder, I gently turn his head with my hand so he can watch. Cameron leans down to meet me, and his lips claim mine.

Usually kissing is just necessary foreplay before the main menu, but Cameron kisses like it's the entire feast. His hand reaches around to grip my waist, his fingertips digging in like he wants to bury them there and never leave. His tongue laps at my mouth, stoking the fires of passion in me, making me dizzy and breathless.

Boone gasps between us, his hardness pressing against mine, and I can only imagine Cameron grinding into him from behind. My hand that's still clutching Boone's face gently caresses his cheek and I move my thumb to brush his soft lips. Cameron breaks away for breath, but he leans his forehead against mine as we pant against Boone's neck. Boone steals my breath this time with tentative licks at my thumb. His lips part as I push my thumb into his wet heat, and he sucks on my digit like he's imagining it's my cock.

Cameron groans in our ears at the sight, and Boone sucks harder.

"Fuck," I say as my cock throbs painfully against my zipper. "Enough."

I step away, delighted by Boone's whimper at the loss of my thumb. With one hand on each of their backs, I direct Boone and Cameron together while I return to the couch for a cushion. Cameron's gaze is all heat and tenderness, and I wonder how he could have grown to feel that much for Boone in such a short time. I feel like we've been teasing at this for the past year, and our connection has grown and strengthened during that time until we were comfortable enough to make this shift. But with Boone, the need to protect and care developed almost immediately. I know that in a relationship like this one, it's okay if your love and feelings for each member are equal yet different. It's to be expected. And what I thought might give me pause, watching Boone and Cameron have a different emotional connection than Cameron and I or even Boone and I, melts away as I watch the tender way they meet and explore one another. It's beautiful.

I return with the cushion and drop it at my feet. The sound startles them out of their embrace, and I lift an eyebrow at Boone and then at the pillow. His nostrils flare at my meaning and he rushes to comply. I hold up a hand to stop him before he sinks to his knees.

"First, you need to be naked. Don't you think, Cam?"

Cameron gets a wicked gleam in his eye as he reaches around Boone from behind and begins to unbutton the man's shirt. Cameron's lips kiss and nip at Boone's neck and lower to his shoulder as fresh skin is revealed. Boone's hands stutter at his belt at the onslaught, and I really ought to help, so I move his hands and tackle his belt myself. Popping the button and lowering the zipper of his jeans reveals a bright red jock strap.

"Oh my God, Cam, he made himself a present. Just for us."

I sink to my knees to divest Boone of his socks and fully remove his pants. My hand travels back up over firm, hairy legs and cups the front of the jock. Cameron's hand reaches down and joins mine, while his other pinches Boone's hard nipple.

"He's plugged himself for us, too," Cameron says with a hoarse voice.

I reach behind and feel the round plastic base and give it a tap. Boone's head falls back against Cameron's shoulder and he lets out a wanton moan.

"He's perfect."

I rise back to my feet, Boone once again sandwiched between us, and lick at the hollow of his throat and then his bobbing Adam's apple. When Boone finally lifts his head and meets my eyes, he doesn't need words. My directions are coming through loud and clear, and he drops to his knees on the cushion like the good boy that he is.

Cameron and I stand over him and he runs a hand over each of us. The visuals right now are almost enough to make me come in my jeans if he rubs too hard. An entranced Cameron, pupils blown wide, me in my tight jeans and see-through chiffon top, and Boone on his knees, naked except for his jock. So fucking hot, my gaze isn't sure where to land.

Boone reaches for Cameron's belt first, so I take the opportunity to unzip and pull my jeans down just enough to get my cock out comfortably. I don't plan on touching myself, but when Cameron's jeans fall to the floor and Boone reaches into his boxers and returns with a dark, dripping, uncut cock, I can't help but grip tight to the base of my own dick.

Holy fuck, Cameron is gorgeous. As Boone pumps him in his fist, the shiny, wet head pokes out more and more until he's fully hard. I have to wipe away the drool from the corner of my mouth as I apparently forgot how to swallow, I'm so mesmerized.

Cameron taps the top of Boone's head. "Don't leave Jay hanging," he says with a nod toward me. I tear my eyes away from Cameron's cock to discover he's been watching me too, and he smirks to let me know he likes what he sees.

Boone reaches out a hand and takes me in his fist. I groan and squeeze my eyes shut as sparks shoot down my spine, collecting in my balls. I'm not going to last long, and I haven't even gotten to test Boone's gag reflexes yet.

Cameron chuckles darkly. "I think you've already broken Jay."

My eyes are still shut but I can tell by his movements that Boone is now watching me too.

"Nope," I say on a groan. "Not broken. Just picturing my Great-aunt Lulu in a nightgown."

"Then come already. You're young. We've got all night," Cameron says, clearly enjoying holding the power at the moment.

"Nope. Not happening. I'm not coming until it's down that one's throat," I say with a nod to Boone.

Cameron's voice gets softer and more demanding as he says, "What are you waiting for, Boone? Make him come."

13

BOONE

I wasn't bullshitting when I said I wasn't worried about our compatibility in the bedroom. If anything, this right here proves it. On my knees, two gorgeous cocks in hand, waiting for me to pleasure them. The only way it will get better is if Jay refuses to let me come again. Or at least makes me wait for it. Then Cameron can come to my aid, make me blow with that gorgeous cock of his in my ass.

So many options. God, I hope I can make this good enough that they'll want to do it again. And again. My jock already has a visible wet spot and my hole clenches around the plug I put in before the date. I thought sex was off the table, according to Cameron's texts anyway, so I had planned on torturing myself with the sexy underwear and plug throughout the evening, then running home to edge myself into oblivion afterwards. But this is so much better.

Cameron's order to take Jay into my mouth makes my cock jump for joy and my head spin. I lick my lips and wrap them around Jay's head, licking and wetting the way with my tongue as I take him farther into my mouth. I move my hand from his base to cup his balls, making a ring with my finger and thumb around the top of them, and squeezing them gently in my palm.

Jay moans, and I slowly slide back off of him and look up. His eyes are shut and his mouth hangs open. One hand clutches at my head while the other grips Cameron's bicep for balance. His grip tightens in my hair and I suck him back down, gagging at first, but then I swallow around him and push farther until my airways are cut off. I swallow again, ripping another moan from him, and pull back enough for a breath before taking him into my throat again.

Cameron's cock jerks in my hand, and I realize I haven't been paying it any attention, I've been so focused on sucking Jay. I squeeze and stroke, and Cameron hums his approval. My knees ache in this position, but that adds to idea that I'm here for their pleasure, and only increases my own.

When I finally get a rhythm going, I bob my head and stroke my fist at the same time, giving both Cameron and Jay the attention they need, until suddenly both of Jay's hands grab at my head. He shoves me down as far as I can go, and though I gag a little at first, I quickly relax and let him shudder his release down my throat. Cameron's cock is forgotten as I cling to Jay's thighs, letting him use my mouth as he chases his pleasure.

When he finally lets up, I slump back onto my heels, lightheaded. Cameron places a gentle hand against my back to steady me, but it's soon gone as he steps around me to catch Jay just as his legs give out. He eases Jay back onto the couch, pulling his pants back up but leaving them undone, and puts down another cushion against the foot of the couch so I can lean back and catch my breath. Cameron curls up next to Jay and dangles an arm down along my chest, soothing and caressing me. He whispers sweet words to both of us, telling us how beautiful we were, how amazing, how sexy.

Another hand joins Cameron's along my chest, and seconds

later, Jay kneels before me. He leans forward and presses his lips against mine in a hard kiss, the kind that demands I pay attention and understand how he feels about what we've just started. I reach for his hand and take it in mine with a squeeze, letting him know I do understand, and I clutch our clasped hands against my chest. Cameron's large hand covers both of ours, and we rest together like that, peaceful and content, with Jay snuggled at my side and Cameron stretched above us.

Eventually, Jay stirs and looks over my head to Cameron.

"I haven't decided yet if this one gets to come," he says with a nod in my direction, and my insides shatter with fireworks of anticipation. "But we need to do something about your predicament."

I turn my head to see Cameron's cock still deep purple and achingly hard. I shift so that I can take him into my mouth, but a hand stops me.

"No, sweetness. Not yet. I think we should move this back to the bedroom."

Cameron strips off his shoes and socks and kicks off his pants and boxers, which were mostly off already. He stands from the couch and holds out a hand to both me and Jay, pulling us up simultaneously from the floor. The muscles bulge under his shirt and a thrill runs through me at how wanton I must have looked, on my knees mostly naked for two clothed men.

Cameron leads the way to his bedroom, still holding our hands like we're teenagers at the mall, not partially dressed men about to fuck each other's brains out. Although I've been here before, this is my first time in Cameron's bedroom. It's not what I imagined based on the living room, which is sleek and sophisticated. This room is warm wood and lots of fluffy pillows and blankets in pastel tones. It looks more like my mother's bedroom, which is not a visual I need right now. Thankfully, when Cameron crawls across the bed and props himself against the headboard, right in the center, all other thoughts flee.

His hard dick bounces and leaves a wet spot on his shirt. Jay must be as mesmerized as I am, because he murmurs, "We need to remedy this situation," and crawls to meet Cameron on the bed. I stand frozen at the foot as I watch Jay slowly divest Cameron of his shirt, running his pale hands over Cameron's dark chest, the most gorgeous contrast of skin I've ever seen. Cameron slides his hands under Jay's sheer shirt, and I can see his hands move across Jay's chest and flick over Jay's nipples. Jay bucks against Cameron, pushing his clothed cock into Cameron's thigh. God, the two of them are so sexy together, I can't help but dig the heel of my palm against my jock, trying to provide any kind of relief to the aching there.

I thought they only had eyes for each other at the moment, but Jay tsks while Cameron nips at his jaw beneath his ear.

"I don't remember giving you permission to touch yourself, Boone. Are you looking to be punished?"

I open my mouth to say, "No," but a moan escapes instead.

Jay still humps against Cameron's thigh and moans too. "God, you both are so sexy. I can't decide which one of you I want to fuck first."

"Me," Cameron says, his voice rough against Jay's throat. "I want to feel you inside me. I'll punish sweetness, here."

Jay grins and places a peck against Cameron's lips. "Perfect. Supplies?"

"Bedside table."

Jay rolls off the bed and sifts through the drawers until he finds the right one.

"Up here, sweetness," Cameron says, moving from his spot and gesturing for me to take it. When I start to sit back, he shakes his head. "Uh-uh. Face the wall, hands on the headboard."

Only for Us

Cameron's strong hands help guide me into the position he wants, and I shiver as he pets me all over. He kneads my shoulders until my head droops between them, I'm so relaxed. He runs a hand along the length of my back, staying away from my sides after a stray touch reveals how ticklish I am. Finally, finally, his hands drift to my ass, kneading and squeezing, pulling my cheeks apart, jostling the plug that has fireworks sparking in my ass, only to push them back together in his sensual massage.

"That doesn't look like punishment to me," Jay teases. "Are you sure you know what you're doing?"

"Are you questioning my skills?" Cameron grips my ass tight and releases it, letting it bounce. He playfully swats the underside, nothing like the punishment Jay was insinuating, but just enough to keep my ass bouncing at his fingertips. Each swat lights a fire inside me, causing the plug to peg my prostate, until there's a bonfire raging in my groin.

The playful spankings stop suddenly, and a tug on the plug sends shivers coursing through me. Cameron gently pulls until my body gives it up. My hole feels empty, clenching around nothing. Two hands spread my cheeks wide and a wet stripe races along my crack. I yelp and buck forward, but strong hands pull me back where a probing tongue awaits.

Little licks trace the starburst of my hole, then press into me. Back and forth, he switches it up, long, wet stripes, tiny kitten licks, and thick, dripping thrusts attack my hole and I moan at the delicious dirtiness of it all. I've rarely gotten rimmed, and never with this amount of fervor. Cameron eats at my hole like it's the most delicious thing he's ever tasted, and I relax and let my brain fog over with pleasure.

14

CAMERON

I could eat out Boone forever. I'm so focused and lost in the desire to drive him mad with pleasure, I forget about Jay behind me. So when a slick finger prods at my opening, combined with a bite on my left cheek, I jolt with surprise. My "oh" vibrates against Boone's hole and he moans louder. The constant stream of noises coming from him hasn't stopped, but every once in a while, I'll do something extra and be rewarded with an increase in volume.

I look over my shoulder and see a naked Jay sitting on his haunches, breathing heavily as he watches his finger circle my hole. I can't watch him too long. My cock hangs heavy between my legs and my balls want so badly to empty, but I want to draw this out as long as I can. When Jay's finger twists inside my entrance, I don't know if I'll make it. I'm tight. It's been well over a year since my ass has seen anything but my own finger or a toy, and the burn of his finger feels amazing.

I return my focus to Boone, trying to calm down a little, but when presented with his flexing hole, I know I'm a goner. I run my finger up and down Boone's crack, letting it drift lower to his taint, and I squeeze his balls for another low moan.

Jay adds another finger and uses his free hand to stroke along my side, helping me relax. He twists his fingers and pegs my prostate, and I groan from the sudden sparks.

"That's right," he says, stroking and twisting and stretching my hole. "Just like that. You're so tight, but you're going to let me in and I'm going to give you what you need."

"Fuck," I growl. "Fuck me already."

I press my flaming cheeks to Boone's spread ones, prodding him more with my tongue to try to ease my embarrassment over how needy I am for Jay's cock. It doesn't help.

Jay chuckles and I hear the rip of a condom wrapper. "So fucking needy. Both of you, on your hands and knees. Asses in the air. You both need this so bad, don't you?"

Lube clicks and a wet tip seeks entrance. I let out a breath against Boone's hole, which sends shivers up his spine but relaxes me enough to let Jay push into me. Slow, steady strokes fill me inch by inch.

"I'm not a virgin." I growl again, my legs shaking from holding myself back from pushing backward and spearing myself on his cock. "You can go faster."

"If you insist," Jay says, promises saturating his voice, dripping like honey.

He pulls back and slams into me, and a brief spear of pain gives way to pleasure and overwhelming sensation as I ride out what he gives me.

Poor Boone whimpers against the headboard. I brace myself against him, my cheek flush with his ass, but I can do no more. My entire focus is taken by Jay and his punishing thrusts.

"Yes, fuck, yes."

"I like it when I make you cuss. I love watching you lose control."

Boone looks beneath him, and moans "Fuck" as he watches my cock bounce hard and fast.

Only for Us

"Boone, help him out," Jay commands, and Boone scrambles from his position to crouch beside me. His hand reaches for my bobbing cock and he squeezes and twists his wrist as he jacks me perfectly in time with Jay's thrusts.

"Not gonna last." The words grit between my clenched teeth. It feels so good, having both of their attentions focused on me. Jay pegs my prostate with every thrust, and my tip drips in Boone's fist.

"Then come, sweetheart. Don't hold back," Jay says, his loving words at odds with the bite on my earlobe. The sharp kick of pain, the ache brought on by his words, the tightening of my balls that I can no longer contain all blend together and I shout out as I spray Boone's fist and my bed with my release.

Jay pulls out and shifts so that I can lie down on my back to recover. He strips himself of the condom and Boone reaches out to him. Boone's hand is still covered in my seed, mixing with Jay's precum as he works Jay's shaft. Slick noises fill the room, combined with heaving breathing, and the knowledge that it's my cum covering Jay's dick right now has my own cock twitching. If I were a few years younger, it would be enough to bring it right back to life.

"Yes," Jay moans, "I'm going to mark you both, so you'll both remember you're mine."

My eyes flit to Boone, who closes his eyes with the most peaceful look spread across his features. This, I think, is what he's waited his whole life for – someone who cares enough to make him his. And Jay, I think, watching as he throws his head back while he empties his balls all over my chest, has been waiting for someone to care for.

And I'm just the lucky son of a gun who gets to watch them both come together.

White puddles on my pecs and drips into my belly button. Boone's fist drips with two loads. It's so hot I want to burn this image into my brain to have for later. Whether things work out between us or not, this is the most erotic moment of my life. One I'm sure will be replayed until I'm too old to get it up.

Jay runs his fingers along my chest, drawing patterns with his cum, then raises his hand to Boone. Boone's tongue darts out and licks Jay's finger clean, and I notice movement in the front of Boone's jock.

"He's been so good for us, Jay. Don't you think Boone deserves a reward?"

Boone gasps as Jay pounces, tackling him down to the bed – into my mess though neither seem to notice – and stripping down his jock with his teeth. Boone's cock smacks Jay's cheek and Jay growls. He leans down and licks a line from Boone's balls all the way up to his tip, then swallows him down. Boone's hips shoot off the bed, and Jay growls again, pinning Boone's hip bones with his palms.

Boone moans and clutches at the bedding, twisting it in his fists. Cum gets smeared everywhere, and I belatedly think how I'm going to have to wash everything before bed.

Worth it.

Boone is so on edge that it only takes a few strokes of Jay's hot mouth before Boone shoots down Jay's throat.

Jay smacks his lips and winks at Boone after he pulls off with a pop.

"Tasty."

"Hngh."

"Uh-oh," I say, leaning down to give Boone a kiss on his forehead. "I think Boone's broken this time."

"That's okay," Jay says and snuggles down behind me, an arm tight around my waist. "We've got all night to put him back together."

I pull Boone to me and wrap around him. I keep waiting for the freak-out to happen, but it doesn't. There might be a twinge of guilt, knowing Dylan would have loved for me to suggest anything like this for us, but back then Dylan was all I wanted. Honestly, he was enough to handle all on his own. But with these two, it feels right. If anything, I'm the superfluous one here, and at some point, they're bound to notice. Until then, I'll enjoy every moment I can get with them.

I murmur, "Sounds perfect. Do you really have a Great-aunt LuLu?"

I feel Jay's snort between my shoulder blades.

15

JAY

I wake feeling like I can't breathe. I'm too warm and there's a heavy weight on top of me. It takes a little too long for my brain to catch up and realize that it's because I'm in bed with two other men, one of which has decided to become my personal blanket.

"Mmph," Cameron grumbles as I try to slip away.

"I have to pee like a race horse," I say, and he loosens his grip.

In his bathroom, all chrome and glass and sleekly modern, I stare at the wide-eyed waif in the mirror. I'm not weirded out that I just participated in a threesome with someone I consider to be a friend. I'm not even weirded out that I just participated in a threesome with someone I previously considered to be an enemy. I'm panicking over the fact that I spent the night with someone. I never do that. No one has ever even considered me sleepover material, much less fought to keep me in bed with them when I tried to get up.

Chances are better than average that I'm going to fuck this up somehow.

I splash cold water onto my face, trying to calm down, but

instead I make myself so cold that I have no option but return to bed and Cameron's warm arms. Unless he's turned over to snuggle Boone in my absence. Then I'll still be cold and alone in bed. Maybe I should just find my clothes and leave.

Cameron startles me, standing outside the door. "Sorry," he says, his voice too sleepy to actually laugh at my surprised squeak. "My turn."

I slide back into bed, keeping to my side, watching Boone's bare back rise and fall in the early morning light. Cameron is back in a flash, lifting the sheets and swatting my ass.

"Scoot over."

I comply, and soon I'm in the middle, the little spoon to Cameron's bigger one. I reach out toward Boone, but I'm afraid of disturbing him, so I pull my hand back.

"You're freaking out, aren't you?" Cameron whispers against my neck.

"A little."

"About us?"

I roll in his hold and wrap an arm around his middle while his arm comes around me and strokes my back. His soft cock lays against his thigh and I can't help but sneak a leg between his, to feel it in all its flaccid glory.

"No," I say into his chest, rubbing my cheek against his nipples. "I've never been in a serious relationship before. I don't know what I'm doing, and I don't want to screw this up."

"The only way you could screw this up is by not communicating. That's the most important thing. It's okay to be scared. It's okay to have doubts. But as long as we share them and talk about them together, then we'll know we did everything we could. It might not work. That's a real possibility with any relationship. But it will be because we don't fit together well, not because any one of us screwed up."

"How do you always know just the right thing to say?"

"I'm a lawyer. It's in the job description."

My stomach growls and I can feel Cameron silently laugh in my arms.

"Sorry. I get up early for work. My stomach is used to being fed by now."

"Then I'll have to do something about that. Stay right here."

I watch the delicious sight of Cameron wandering around his room naked, pulling clothes from his dresser and unfortunately covering up in pajama pants and a t-shirt.

"I don't think you'd fit in my pants," he whispers, and hands over a long sweatshirt that falls to my knees when I put it on.

"I had no idea you were such a giant," I laughingly say as he helps me roll up my sleeves, then leads me into his kitchen.

"My sister bought it for me years ago," he says as he digs through his cabinets and pulls out a skillet. "She apparently thinks I'm a lot bigger than I really am, but I couldn't get rid of it."

I huff and put my hands on my hips. "So you're a heroic lawyer, great friend, and now you're also a terrific brother. Oh, and you bowl. Is there anything you can't do?"

Cameron looks up from where he's digging in the fridge for bacon and eggs and gives me a solar-powered smile.

"I can't bake. I can't knit. And I can't for the life of me figure out how to turn this sterile apartment into a home as cozy and welcoming as yours."

"Oh."

I feel my neck get warm, and hopefully he puts it down to the sweatshirt and not how embarrassingly pleased I am that he liked my home.

"Can I help?"

He turns from the stove and the skillet where he's laid out strips of bacon. "Do you want some toast? You could start with that. See? I share my kitchen. No imaginary do-not-cross lines here."

I stick out my tongue, which he pretends to bite at, and wander into his kitchen. It's as sleek as the rest of his house, but small. I don't think I'd like to do a lot of cooking in this space either.

I man the toaster oven, making toast the way my grandmother used to, with lots of butter on first before laying it flat in the oven so the butter gets all melted and warm and gooey. Boone shuffles out of the room completely naked. He rubs at his hair and blinks at the light. I had no idea how adorable he would look when he first woke up.

"If you need something to wear," Cameron says, keeping a hand on the skillet while turning to address Boone, "I can grab you something."

"Yeah, that would be good." Boone's soft voice can barely be heard over the popping of the bacon.

"Watch this for me?" Cam asks me and I switch places with him.

"Do you like your bacon crispy or soft?"

"Soft, like I like my men." He looks back and forth between Boone and me. "Hmm, or at least soft on the inside." He waggles an eyebrow at me before he leads Boone back to the bedroom.

I pull out half the bacon onto a paper-towel-covered plate Cameron already had prepared and leave the rest to get crispy, the way that I like them.

"Do either of you have plans for the day? I was thinking we could do something together," Cam says, returning with a t-shirt-and-sweats-clad Boone in tow. He loads up a plate with food and grabs a stool at the counter.

"As long as it isn't bowling," I say.

"What about hiking?" Boone asks. He sits next to Cam and steals food off his plate until I slide a plate of his own across the counter to him. "There's a nice trail along Horsetooth that I like."

"That sounds like fun," Cameron says, taking a bite of his bacon and distracting me for a brief second. Very brief.

"What in the hell have I gotten myself into? Do I look like I hike to you?" I wave a hand down my sweatshirt-clad body, which makes me look even more like a little kid than I already do. I can't put on muscle for shit, no matter how hard I've tried. So I finally gave up and decided that exercise and I will never be good friends, and we parted ways a long time ago. Bowling and sex are the closest I've come in years.

Cameron and Boone share a smile, but I can promise that they aren't going to talk me into joining them.

"Hiking can be one of those Cam-Boone things you do together. Special time for just the two of you. Trust me. I'm thrilled at the idea."

I take a bite of crispy bacon and then wrap it and some egg into a folded piece of toast. I'm squirmy for some reason this morning, so I stay standing in the kitchen, which honestly is usually how I eat my breakfast anyway.

"Actually, that does bring up a point," Boone says, setting down his toast and chewing on his lip instead. "Should we set some sort of rule? Like we only do things when it can be all three of us?"

"No, I trust you both," I say and realize with a shock that I mean it. I think Boone looks even more shocked.

"Me too," Cameron says. "And as for today, we could stay in. Watch a movie."

"Netflix and chill?" I ask with a wink. "Sounds like a great idea, but I think we've already done plenty of chilling."

"I was thinking more like Hulu and commit," Cam says with a happy sigh.

By the time Monday morning rolls around, it feels like I've always been a part of this threesome. It comes that naturally. Even after we parted ways Saturday afternoon, we still texted in a group chat, keeping each other company the rest of the weekend, even with things as mundane as what we were eating or watching on television. Cameron had a keen interest in what I was baking, and feigned disappointment when I told him I was catching up on my knitting, and not baking anything new for him.

Kieran stops by at four to pick me up so we can work on floral arrangements. He promised something to Craig last weekend, but I was so wound around the axle of my crazy love life – holy shit, I actually have a love life – that I had to postpone until today. Craig will just have to be satisfied with seeing everything a day or two late. Sometimes, sharing ownership of a best friend can be really annoying.

"Cameron was certainly in a good mood today at work," Kieran says as I drop into the passenger side seat. "You wouldn't know anything about that, would you?"

"Why would I?" I say, keeping my eyes firmly on the road. We haven't discussed telling anyone else about our relationship yet. Boone is barely out, and Cameron is still very much seen as a grieving boyfriend, so it might reflect poorly on either of them. I have a feeling our crowd of friends would expect that kind of behavior from me, though.

"Well, he briefly mentioned another date with that Boone guy, but then your name kept cropping up. Odd, huh?"

"Yep. No idea."

Still, I love hearing that our weekend put Cameron in a good mood. Me too. So good that even Larry informing me that his wife found my muffins charming but a little too rustic for the coffee house couldn't ruin my day.

Our first stop is a thrift store where Kieran and I scour over old-fashioned bottles – or maybe just old-looking ones – and pick our favorites. The ones I pick have patterns etched into the glass, flowers and lacy designs. Kieran prefers the ones that are more geometric and molded into different shapes and colors. Together, though, they'll look terrific.

Next, we go to the wholesale florist and pick some simple flowers from the list that Craig gave to Kieran. We choose softly colored flowers – roses of course, but also snapdragons and astilbes, ones that give a slightly more rustic air. I suppose Mrs. Larry was right, but if she thinks rustic is an insult, that's her problem.

Kieran loads up a basket full of individual stems into his car and we unpack everything onto his and Ted's dining room table. Ted's in the kitchen cooking dinner and invites me to stay.

I brought a bag of twine and ribbon, and I show Kieran how I imagined the centerpieces – different bottles clumped together, each with a single stem, and a ribbon tied around each one. He snaps off pictures of the different variations that I work with from the options we've selected and sends them to Craig.

"Thanks for doing this, man," Kieran says, slumping into a chair after his phone dings with hearty praise and promises that he and Zach will pick their favorites so we can compile a shopping list for the final reception table count. "I never thought being a best man would be so difficult. I mean, I thought a topless bar was the extent of it, and since we obviously wouldn't have that, I'd be getting off scot-free. Who knew a wedding was such work?"

"Wedding planners, probably," I say, smiling my thanks to Ted as he sets steaming bowls of veggie linguini in front of

Kieran and me. He returns a second later with a bowl for himself.

"You're very talented," Ted says, twisting his pasta around his fork and nodding to the kitchen. "You should see how well your herbs are doing. In fact, we're partaking of some of your basil tonight."

"Aww, I'm so glad you liked it. And that I didn't kill the herbs before getting them to you and your green thumb."

We finish dinner, chatting aimlessly about the wedding and work. Ted and Kieran are as adorable together as ever, but for the first time, my chest doesn't clench at the sight of them. Maybe, just maybe, I finally have something of my very own.

16

BOONE

Boone: Do you think we could get together and talk later?

I reread the text four times before finally pressing send. Despite all my hesitation I get an almost instantaneous reply.

Jay: Sure! Want to come to mine at 4?

To be honest, I could see how Jay fit into my life sexually, but not emotionally, until recently. Maybe it's because every time he spoke to me it made my dick hard, but he has that kind of take-charge attitude that I've come to rely on in all areas, not just the bedroom.

I arrive promptly at four at a small house on the outskirts of Old Town. Jay answers the door in yoga pants that highlight his package and a tank top with one strap sliding down his shoulder. I reach out to fix it, a single finger caressing his pale shoulder, which causes an obvious movement in the front of his pants.

"So, was 'talk' some sort of really bad euphemism? Because I know we agreed that we all didn't have to be together for something to happen, but I know Cameron would enjoy watching me punish you for not being straightforward with me."

I gulp at the tone of his voice and let his words sink in.

"No! I mean, I really do want to talk. You're just ..."

As I swallow heavily again, weighing the imagined results of my halted word choice, Jay pins me with a raised eyebrow.

"Straightforward. Remember?"

"So pretty," I whisper on a sigh.

Jay smiles and throws the door open farther, allowing me to enter.

"As much as I love watching you get flustered, I don't want my neighbors to complain. Sit," he says and points to a couch covered in colorful throws and pillows. "I'll grab us drinks."

I sit like I'm told and run my hands along the knitted blanket underneath me. My aunt made me a blanket when I was younger that used to lay across the foot of my bed, but it was rough and scratchy and a horrible yellow. I never used it, but my mom wouldn't let me get rid of the thing. Jay's blanket is nothing like that. The yarn is like a baby lamb under my hands, soft and comforting, and the colors are jewels to decorate his boring, but very cushy, brown couch. It's an interesting side to the man who I think of as all teasing and torment.

"You like the blanket then?"

See, teasing.

Jay sets two cups of freshly made coffee in front of us, and I notice a little milk has already been added to mine, just like I order it at the coffee house.

"It's soft," I say, like an idiot, because of course he knows his own blanket is soft. If I were to ever become sick, I think this is where I'd want to recover. Jay's couch. But that would sound even weirder to say to him.

"Mmm," he says, taking a quick sip. "Good yarn costs a fortune, but it's worth it. There's a place here in town that even teaches you how to spin your own. Can't you just see me at a spinning wheel, making my own yarn?"

I consider him over my coffee. It isn't a picture I would have thought of before, but after looking around his home and seeing the bigger picture, I'd have to say I could.

"Yeah. I had no idea you were so crafty, but yeah, I can totally see it."

"Well, it would be fun," he says, almost apologetically, and grips his mug as if he needs something to cling to. "So, what's up? Why did you want to not euphemistically talk?"

"Is euphemistically a word?"

"If it isn't, it is now. Stop trying to stall. Spill."

I set down my mug and settle back into the couch. Running my hands along the blanket again somehow gives me courage. "I don't know what to do with my life."

Jay puts down his own mug and turns until he's facing me. He lifts one of my roving hands and twines it together with his, stroking his other hand gently over the top, effectively sandwiching mine. My breathing slows to match the movements of his hand, and only then do I realize that I was almost hyperventilating when I spoke.

"First," he says, still gently reassuring me with his hands, "remember there is no judgement here. I do not and could not think anything less of you because of what you just admitted. There is nothing wrong with that."

A knot of insecurity that had formed between my shoulder blades loosens with his words.

"And second, I'm honored that you came to me with this. Don't get me wrong, I have no clue why you picked me over Cameron, but you have no idea how much it flatters me."

"I get the feeling Cameron had his shit together from the time he was a toddler. Can't you imagine baby Cameron toddling around with a briefcase and tie?" I smile then replay my words and try to pull back in horror, but Jay holds tight to my hand. "Not that I think you don't have your shit together!"

"Relax, sweetie. I understand what you mean. Cameron's put-togetherness can be a little intimidating. Besides, barista and failed muffin man isn't exactly what I dreamt of putting on my resume as a child."

His wistful smile has me mentally kicking myself. Making Jay sad was the last thing I wanted to do.

"Sorry," I say and duck my head, focusing on the way our fingers blend together, without an obvious beginning or end.

Jay releases my hand and turns my head to his with a hand on either side of my jaw. His blue-green eyes flash with feeling and he pecks a kiss to my lips before speaking.

"Hey, if we're going to do this, there's no sorry. There's no watching what we say around each other. It's hard to offend me. I've got a tough skin. So, we say what we mean and we accept each other for it. Or we don't. But no sorries. If I hear another one out of your mouth, I may have to punish you later for it."

I clutch my suddenly free hands together against my lap as my brain supplies all sorts of visuals for his words. Jay bending me over and spanking me. Jay making me stand naked in a corner. Jay sitting on top of me like before, exploding his seed across my body and not letting me come.

"So–" Jay grins like he knows where my mind went. I have no idea what we were talking about anymore. I'm still stuck on punishments. His grin deepens at my confusion, and he supplies, "Your future."

Right. The fact that I don't have one. I breathe deep.

"Remember, no judgements," Jay says as if he can read minds as well as he does bodies.

"I always planned on going to the NFL." It almost sounds silly now when I say it. Like a five-year-old's dream, not one of a serious adult. "From age eight until age twenty-one, it was all football, all the time."

Jay's face remains amazingly neutral. I still love football and even I want to wrinkle my nose at how single-minded I was back then.

"Then after my injury, things went to shit. The car dealership snapped me up because they liked the idea of a local sports hero on staff, and I went along with it because it was easier than actually figuring out what I wanted."

Jay's hand returns to mine while he props his other arm against the back of the couch and leans onto it.

"Did you like the car dealership?"

"No," I say without hesitation. "But it made my dad reasonably happy. 'Lots of sports figures open dealerships when they retire. It's a start.'" I imitate his deep, gruff voice and Jay scoots closer by an inch. "It wasn't what I wanted to do."

"And what was that?"

"I have no idea. I still have no idea what I want to do."

"When you were younger, what was your backup plan?" I frown at him, and he adds, "You know, what you wanted to do in case your dreams of playing professionally didn't come true."

My laugh startles him.

"My dad didn't allow for backup plans."

Jay narrows his eyes like he's thinking, and then shifts on the couch. A leg swings across mine, and before I can blink, Jay straddles my lap. The weight feels so good, my hips jerk forward of their own volition.

"Uh-uh," Jay says, his lithe hands holding my hips, propelling him forward until I can feel his breath against my chin. "Surely, at some point growing up, you must have had dreams for yourself. Even if you knew they could never happen. Didn't you dream?"

Of course I did, but they're buried so deep I'm not sure I even know how to uncover them.

"You did," he says, letting up and bracing his hands on my chest instead of my hips. "I can see it in your face."

I still have no idea how he manages it, but a sly grin spreads across his face.

"I'll tell you what. I'll let you grind against me all you want. You can even come. As long as you tell me what your dreams used to be."

Jay scoots forward and presses his groin against mine, and I groan.

"Nope, no groans," he says, clearly enjoying my torture. "Only words. I'll even start you out. What was the very first thing you can remember wanting to be? You know, when you're still in preschool and you have the craziest ideas of what is possible. For me, it was a zookeeper and Wonder Woman. Zookeeper would have been my secret identity, obviously."

He's so earnest, I know he's telling me the truth, and I love him for it. I can't even laugh at its ridiculousness, because I can just imagine how dearly young Jay wanted those things.

"A cop. When I was little, I wanted to be a cop. I wanted to help people. But my dad said only losers who couldn't make it to college became cops."

Jay's face takes on a hard edge, but his voice is soft when he says, "Cops are not losers. The world needs more good men who are policemen. Can you imagine being a cop now? Close your eyes and think about it."

I follow his orders, because of course I do. But I can't picture myself as a cop. I like the idea of helping people still, but I don't like the idea of ever being violent, even though it might be necessary. I got enough of that on the football field, and it wasn't what I liked about the sport.

Jay grinds into me and I press back. My dick hardens as we

rub against each other, and he grabs my hands and wraps them around him until my hands cup his ass. It flexes in my palms, and the room is suddenly too hot.

"Keep talking," Jay growls in my ear.

"No," I say when I can remember. "No cop. But I still like the thought of helping people."

"What was your degree?"

The throbbing in my pants grows heavier and heavier, and I'm panting when I say, "General business. With a minor in education."

My parents didn't know about the education minor, but with my plans to start a camp for kids once I became an NFL player, I thought it might be an asset.

Oh.

"I wanted to start a sports camp for underprivileged or maybe even LGBT youth. You know how lots of sports figures start charities and things? I used to daydream about what I would do when I became famous."

"So, you like sports, you like kids, you want to make a difference, and you have a degree in education. I think we're finally getting somewhere."

Jay leans forward and nips at my earlobe. The pressure and rhythm of our dicks pressed together through our clothes increases as he licks his way down my neck. His muscles tense and release in my hands at a faster speed, and my breathing increases to match.

Jay's body is heaven and the way he makes me feel is perfect. When I buck up against him, he doesn't complain or chastise me for no longer talking. He presses back harder, and says, "Good boy. You've been so good, sharing yourself with me, you've earned a reward."

Jay's hands explore under my shirt until they reach my nipples. He bites underneath my ear as he tugs and pulls on my sensitive nubs, and I can't hold back any longer. My balls draw up and I explode into my briefs as he twists my nipples with such force I can't tell which is pain and which is ecstasy. It draws on forever, or at least until my vision goes black and sparkly, and I crash my head against the back of the couch in a daze.

"Such a good boy," I hear whispered in my ear before I pass out.

17

CAMERON

"We've made reservations for the second week in June. Does that work for you?" Celeste asks.

"Of course," I say. "I'll start planning now. What do you think the kids would like to do best?"

I turn the phone on speaker and open up my calendar to mark down the dates.

"What dates?"

"Thursday through Wednesday." That means I won't be able to go to Zach and Craig's wedding, which is okay because I was mostly going for Kieran. I don't know either groom very well. "And I want them out of doors as much as possible. They're looking a little like zombies these days."

"Then I guess taking them to my friend's video game store is out of the question?"

"Such a funny guy. Don't make me pull out my mom voice."

"Fine. You're no fun," I say, keeping the phone on speaker and heading into the kitchen. Boone and Jay are coming over for dinner later and I still have the dishes from breakfast sitting out. "I've got to go get things cleaned up, but I'll do some research and send you some ideas, okay?"

"Why do you have to clean up? Are you having a guest? Are you finally getting back out there, Cammy?"

"Talk to you soon. Bye!"

I slam the end call button before she can say anything else. The only thing worse than a nosy sister is a nosy sister getting all judgmental about you seeing two guys. That's a discussion I'd like to stave off for as long as humanly possible.

It's been four days since I've seen either Boone or Jay, although they both saw each other earlier in the week. They each texted me their own versions of how their afternoon went, but the thought of Jay dry-humping Boone until he came in his pants makes me hard every time I think about it. I've taken a few extra showers this week as a result.

There's no jealousy, not that I thought there would be. I'm not even sorry that I wasn't there to enjoy it in person, because I love that they had some special time to themselves. As long as they tell me about it, because imagining it is half the fun, then I'm happy that things are going so well between them. I know Boone was nervous about Jay forgiving him, but I think he's finally getting to the point now where he understands that it is all in the past.

My thoughts travel to Dylan, as they so often do whenever I think about the two men in my life. Sometimes I worry that I shouldn't be so lucky. To have had a great love, and then to find not just another, but two others, that could turn into something truly special. It seems like too much for one person to be allowed. Like I've already met my happiness quotient.

But then I think back on all of our times together, and all the stories of his times in California before we met. If anyone lived life to the fullest, it was Dylan. If anything, I was the one who was too serious, staying at home and studying while he went out and partied. Maybe this is just me catching up.

Although if that were the case, if this is just my version of an early midlife crisis, then why do I *feel* so much? Why am I spending hours at home today to make sure that everything is perfect for dinner here tonight?

With the kitchen clean, I go about setting the dining room table – something I rarely use for more than an extra work desk – for dinner. I got some flowers at the grocery store for the table, and I snip off a rose for each of their plates.

I'm not much of a chef, but I have a recipe for tequila lime tilapia that friends always enjoyed when Dylan and I entertained back in California. With the fish in the oven and rice in the rice cooker, I have a few minutes free to shower and get ready.

Daydreams of Jay and Boone have run through my head all day and as I soap up my body, my dick reminds me he's been almost as eagerly awaiting this evening as I have. But no, I don't have the return power that these younger boys do, and I don't want to risk wasting my shot on the shower floor.

I rinse as quickly as I can, and with the water off, a rhythmic rap at the door echoes down the hall. With the towel draped around my waist, I rush to the front door and peek through the peephole. I can feel the heat in my cheeks as I open the door, hiding behind it so the neighbors won't get a shock, and let Jay and Boone in.

My eyes dart to the kitchen clock, which reads five 'til six.

"I think we should make a rule that this is how you will always answer the door," Jay teases with a waggle of his eyebrows and a saucy finger leaving tingles behind in a trail down my still-dripping chest.

Boone nod as he licks his lips, and I love how both of my men show their appreciation in such fun and different ways. I could eat them both up this instant, but then that would ruin all my hard work.

"Hang on, it's later than I realized. I'll go change and then we can finish dinner together."

"Must you?" Jay asks with a fake pout and leans a chin on Boone's shoulder. "Tell him, Boone. Give him those puppy dog eyes so he won't take away our view."

Boone does his best, but there is no way I am cooking the rest of dinner in only a towel.

"I'll be right back."

"Meanie," Jay says, and they both kick off their shoes and leave them by the front door.

I return in a pair of comfortable slacks and my favorite button-down shirt. I never wear it for work, because it always turns me on a little, the way the ultra-soft fabric feels against my skin. It's a lovely shade of peach, too, which I know highlights my skin tone, at least according to my sister, Celeste.

I pull out the cutting board and start to chop up a mix of squash and zucchini. Jay and Boone sit at stools on the other side of the counter, but Boone leans forward to watch my movements.

"Can I do anything to help?" he asks, his eyes flickering to mine, and he sits back with a blush.

"You can open the wine. Or beer. I bought both, so whatever you want to drink. Check the fridge."

Boone pulls out the Riesling I bought to pair with the fish and I pass him the opener. Jay stays across the counter, flipping lazily through my stack of mail, then stills. He flicks at the corner of what I can tell is the invitation to Zach and Craig's wedding. "You were invited too? I was thinking we might all go together. You know, let everyone know about us for the first time."

My family drives me crazy on the best of days. Look up overprotective and worrywart in the dictionary and there was probably a competition over which female MacGowan to feature –

Celeste or Mom. I need some time to ease them into the idea of me seeing someone else after Dylan, and then a little more for my own sanity for the hysteria waiting when I tell them I'm seeing two someones.

"I can't. I've got work," I say, too quickly, and I curse myself for not being able to come up with a better excuse. It doesn't go unnoticed.

"On a Saturday?"

"There's a lawyer association thing in Denver. I'd already sent my regrets."

"Oh," Jay says, trying to hide his disappointment. "Well, would you like to go with me, Boone?"

Boone's smile shines bright as he pours wine into glasses and carries them over to the dining table. "Of course. I'd love to," he says, and busses a kiss against Jay's cheek when he returns to the kitchen.

It seems to appease Jay a little, but he still frowns at the invitation in his hand.

"Go grab your plates," I tell them. "Dinner is about ready."

As I sauté the vegetables quickly in a pan, they return to the kitchen, and Jay has tucked his rose behind his ear. I serve his plate and hand it back to him with a kiss to his sensitive ear, just below the flower. He hums his approval.

When Boone approaches, I reach for his plate but he scrunches his eyebrows at me.

"I can serve myself," he says, with humor in his voice.

"I'm well aware," I tell him and keep a grip on the plate until he finally releases it to my control. "Maybe it's silly and I'm rushing, this only being our second date and all," I say louder so Jay can hear me too, "but I want to spoil both of you tonight. Take care of you."

Boone's eyes widen, but he allows me to serve his dinner and carry his plate back to the dining table for him. After I grab my own plate and return to the table with my helping, Boone points an opinionated fork in my direction.

"Technically, it's the fourth date for you and me. And you've been friends with Jay for much longer, so I don't think anyone is rushing into anything here – physically or emotionally."

He raises an eyebrow for me to challenge him, but his earnest assurance soothes my nervous heart. Boone might not be the most vocal of men, but he gives his opinion when he really feels it.

"What he said," Jay says, then pops a bite of food into his mouth. "This is really good. I had no idea you could cook."

"I don't much. Just a few dishes that I know are decent. I'm not one of those people who can enter a kitchen and magically turn anything in the pantry into a delicious meal."

"It's better than me," Boone says with twinkling eyes. "I burnt a pot black once trying to boil water."

"Is that even possible?" I ask at the same time as Jay says, "Oh, honey."

"But I know all the best places for delivery. I do bring something to the table." Boone laughs at his own pun.

"Sweet cheeks, you bring so much more than that to the table, you practically light the table on fire."

Boone ducks his head at Jay's flattery, which isn't really flattery at all, but the God's honest truth. Boone could set the whole apartment on fire with his innocent eroticism. That sweetness that's just begging to be corrupted. Mix that with Jay's flaming-hot dominance, and it's a wonder my building is still standing.

"What about you?" I ask Jay, trying to take some of the attention away from Boone and give him a breather. "Where did you learn to cook like you do?"

"Oh, I'm not much for cooking, but I do love to bake. I learned from my grandmother. She would let me help make the breads and desserts at family get-togethers. No one else ever wanted to help. My brother was always too busy on his phone and my mom considered it her only time off. But I love the smell of baking bread or the spiced scent of pies in the air. I love the way it feels in your hands, and how it's by feel that you know if something is right or not. Plus, it gave me time with her that was just for us, and she never once made me feel weird about the fact that I was a boy who liked being in the kitchen with her. She made me feel like I belonged there." Jay shakes his head, clearing the dazed quality his eyes had taken on. "Sorry. Didn't mean to drone on."

"No, I love hearing about it," Boone says, and I nod my agreement. "My dad would have yelled the house down if I had tried to hang with my mom in the kitchen. I want to hear more stories like that. They make me happy."

My chest aches for Boone. My family was always very accepting of me, no matter what it was that I wanted – whether it be law school or to love a man. Jay hasn't talked about his family much, but I get a similar impression from him. I try to keep it from angering me. That won't do anyone any good now, and it will only bring the evening down.

"Speaking of making you happy …" Jay says and stands from the table. His Cheshire grin gets wider the more Boone and I look confused. Then he turns around and flounces out of the room.

18

BOONE

"I got you a present," Jay says when he returns, setting a small box onto Cameron's dining table. He shoots me a sly smile that turns wicked. "Actually, I suppose it's more like a present for us, and torture for you."

He winks at Cameron, and Cameron's boisterous laugh fills the room. My skin prickles with heat.

"Aren't you going to open it?" Cameron teases me into action.

My body is already a contradiction of reactions, hot and embarrassed at their teasing, excited and pulsing that Jay thought about me and bought me something. I pull at the bow and open the lid.

Fuck. My breathing stutters and my hands shake. The heat pulsing through my veins is pure delicious torture, more of which I know is coming, based on the metal cage shining under the fancy pendant lights hanging in the dining room.

"Well?" Cameron asks, but my limbs won't respond, so he leans over for a peek. "Jesus, Jay."

"I know. I have the best ideas." He spears a piece of zucchini with his fork and pops it in his mouth with a flourish. "I was thinking we could lock him up and take turns with him while he's frustrated and aching. Eventually, we can get tested, and see how many loads we can fill him with before we give in and let him come. Or we could cage him and plug him but only play with each other while he watches. So many options, and each one has my dick hard."

A foot travels from my knee to my crotch, feeling how embarrassingly hard I already am at the thought.

Jay pats his foot against my zipper. "Ooh, and I'm not the only one."

Cameron scoots his chair back and wraps his arms around me, kissing my temple. "Don't tease the poor dear."

"He loves it."

I really do. I've simply forgotten how to use my words to tell them so. Thankfully, my dick does it for me. Cameron trails a hand down my chest to my straining pants and Jay's foot. He presses his palm and Jay's toes further into my groin while he nibbles on my ear. A whimper escapes and I bite down on my lip.

"I know." Jay snaps his fingers in front of my face, startling me out of my pleasurable daze. "We'll cage him, turn him over, and eat dessert off his ass."

At this point, they could do whatever the fuck they wanted to me and I'd be happy, but Cameron barks out a laugh. "Boone might have something to say about that one."

Boone does, and it is *yes, please.*

"Unfortunately, I don't care what he has to say about it. That's the beauty of being a bossy fucker." Jay's lips purse and his eyes twinkle at all the wicked thoughts rushing through his brain. "Tell me you wouldn't want to lick whipped cream from his hole."

"I'm beginning to see your point. Tell me more," Cameron says, still massaging my crotch and Jay's foot together. If they're going to try to get me into that cage, they're going about it all wrong. There's no way I'll deflate enough to fit any time soon between his ministrations and Jay's dirty talk.

"First, we need to fit him with the cage."

"He's so hard. How do you propose we do that?"

Glad I'm not the only one to notice.

Jay's foot drops and he leans forward in his chair, locking eyes with me.

"We're going to make him come." Oh God. "But Boone?"

I lick my lips to get my mouth working, but still only manage an, "Uh-huh?"

"Enjoy it, because this is the only time you'll get to come tonight."

My groan is drowned out by the scraping of my chair as Cameron pulls it away from the table. Jay drops to the ground and I watch as he fucking crawls on his hands and knees under the table to me. The staccato breath at the back of my neck tells me Cameron finds Jay's advance as sexy as I do, his hand stilling its torture as we watch with bated breaths.

The rose behind his ear gets lost somewhere along the way, though I'm surprised I notice with those green-blue eyes sparkling on the same level as my crotch. When the lithe blond settles between my legs, and my dick jerks its notice, he slowly rolls down one of my dress socks. I wore my nicest shoes tonight since Cameron's apartment seems to demand it. A nibble at my big toe startles me, and had Cameron not pulled my chair out I would have banged my knee hard against the underside of the table.

Jay giggles and yanks my foot back to his mouth, making little nips at the pads of each toe. I've never had a foot fetish, but I'm so on edge right now everything feels erotic, even the tiny licks to my toes.

Cameron has disposed of my shirt before I even realize

what's happening, and he stands behind me, plucking at my nipples while he watches Jay torture my toes.

"Get down here and help me, Cam," Jay says, finally releasing one foot only to move on to the other.

"But I'm enjoying the view." Cameron's voice tickles the back of my neck, giving me goosebumps.

"Wouldn't you rather enjoy the view with his cock in your mouth?"

Yes. Yes, please.

I love the teasing, but if Jay is right and this is the only time I'm going to come tonight, I want to experience their mouths again. Then, I'll be caged and used for their pleasure only. It sounds so wrong and so perfect, all at once.

"I think he likes the sound of that." Cameron's laugh ruffles my hair, and then he's gone, kneeling on the ground near Jay. Dear God, the sight of the two of them together.

Like he can read my mind, Cameron leans over to Jay. With a slow smile, eyes firmly watching as Jay trembles as he nears, Cameron devours Jay's mouth. The normally bossy man is reduced to a quivering mess as Cameron takes what he needs like he's sipping his desires from Jay's lips.

Cameron slips a hand around my ankle, stroking my calf to let me know I haven't been forgotten. When he breaks away from a dazed Jay, he turns his satisfied smirk on me.

"Lift up," he orders, and by the time I comply, my slacks are open and yanked down my body along with my briefs in a swift motion. Once again, I'm naked while Jay and Cameron are still fully clothed. I should feel embarrassed, but that only makes it hotter.

Hands caress my legs and stroke my inner thighs as my legs are spread wider to straddle the chair. My cock juts out to greet them with a pearl of precum filling my slit as they situate themselves, each near a leg.

Jay leans forward to lick a stripe up my shaft, but only on one side. His eyes never leave Cameron's. A ragged breath parts Cameron's lips and he bends to give attention to his side. Their tongues slide along my length, sometimes twirling together, other times just ensuring that every square inch of tight, sensitive skin is dripping with their saliva. More precum drips, but they leave my slit alone, like it's the precious final treat and they haven't decided which one should get it.

Jay moves back a fraction, his long, thin fingers reaching underneath to cup my balls, making my cock jut out even further as he presses against my taint while he gently squeezes.

"You first, I insist," he says to Cameron with a wink, and Cameron doesn't hesitate to swallow me down.

A shout punches out of my chest, but Cameron's strong hands on my hip and thigh keep me from thrusting too far into his mouth. As his hot mouth surrounds me and his tongue milks my shaft, Jay's tongue begins to slaver at the tight skin of my balls, coating them with as much spit as my dripping dick.

"What's it called when you switch out players in sports?" Jay looks at Cameron with a crease between his brows.

Cameron releases me and I hold back a whimper. "How should I know?" He laughs. "I'm not a sports guy."

Two heads turn to me, innocent and questioning, while my cock proudly jerks between them, begging for attention.

"Sub-out," I say, the clear desperation in my voice causing them both to smile.

Jay taps Cameron on the top of the head. "Sub-out," he says, and dips forward to taste my cock.

My laugh turns into a groan as he hollows out his cheeks around me.

They bob their heads back and forth, one after another, taking turns as my head hits their throats until it's too much.

"Oh! I'm gonna–"

Cameron locks his lips around me and swallows as I pulse into his throat. My head swims with the pleasure, and I close my eyes as the last drops drain from me.

The sensation that pulls me back to myself is the feeling of cold metal clasping closed around my spent cock. My eyes snap open to see Jay fitting the cage into place and handing the key to Cameron, who places a soft kiss on the end of the metal.

A sweet gesture, but one I can't even feel.

19

CAMERON

"I decided which of your fantasies I want to try first," I tell Jay, leaning over and letting him taste Boone on my tongue. I pocket the key to the cock cage and give my pants a happy pat.

I could kiss Jay forever, but then we wouldn't get to any of the rest of the fun.

"You and me," I say against his swollen lips. "I want you to fuck me while Boone watches, and then, when he almost can't stand it anymore, we're going to turn him over and let me fuck him while you're inside me."

Jay mouths at my chin and jaw until he gets to the spot before my ear that drives me crazy.

"I like the way you think. Who'd have thought you'd have such a dirty mind, counselor? Especially when you usually have such a clean mouth."

He isn't the first one to tease me about my lack of cussing. My mom would have literally washed my mouth out, and then when I got older, it seemed so superfluous. But Jay certainly had a way of bringing it out in me.

I extend my hand to Boone, who rises from the dining chair

on shaky legs, and help him to the bedroom. Leaving the main lights off, I turn on a corner lamp to give us enough light to see each other but not be too overwhelming. I fluff two pillows and once he is resting comfortably, I hand him a bottle of lube.

"Feel free to prepare yourself while I focus my attentions on Jay."

Jay laughs and leans over Boone on the bed until Boone stares at him with wide eyes. "Get your hole wet and ready. I want you fucking yourself with three fingers by the time Cameron's ready for you."

Boone's pupils are blown wide by Jay's dirty instructions, and all he can do is swallow hard in response.

"Oh, sweetness," I say, pressing a kiss against the side of his mouth. "You are so perfect for us."

Jay tugs at my hand and leads me to the end of the bed. He pulls at my collar until I lean down for a kiss. His lips are fierce and demanding, showing me how much he's wanted this, so I return the favor. I have wanted Jay for months, but I wasn't ready. Not until Boone showed me I wasn't a monster for moving on so quickly. I honestly wouldn't be here without either one of them, and I'm so fucking grateful.

I pour every ounce of gratitude I can into my return kisses. I fumble to remove his clothing, wanting to feel his bare, tight flesh under my hands. Jay's body is thin and pale and beautiful. I stroke both hands down his sides to his waistband, and I think I could probably span his waist with both of my hands. I'd rather strip him naked than bother to find out. I release his mouth and breathlessly lower myself to nibble at his flat stomach while I grapple with his button and zipper. His stomach heaves in and out, displaying his own breathlessness, and I hurry to expose the rest of him. I bite at his jutting hip bones and cup both cheeks in my hands when I finally get his pants down to his ankles.

Jay's cock leaks against my cheek as I take in the warm,

musky skin at the crease between his groin and his thigh. I want to inhale his scent and remember it forever. Jay whines each time I nuzzle into him, pressing his cock against my face, urging me to take him in. I decide to torture him a bit longer, since he seems to enjoy torturing others, and tongue his balls before sucking one side and then the other into my mouth.

"Cam, fuck!" he shouts, and I grin, rolling them and batting them lightly with my tongue before pulling off.

I swirl a tongue around his beautiful mushroom head and lick the dripping tip before sliding my lips around him. My hands find my own buckle and zipper and I expose my hard cock, slowly rubbing myself while I enjoy the taste of Jay in my mouth.

"Hands and knees, Cameron," Jay says, patting at my head. "I'm not going to bust until I'm deep inside you."

I finish undressing as I arrange myself on the bed at Boone's feet. And what a sight he's giving me. Boone has one knee up and the other leg kicked out so he can reach his own hole. Two fingers spear in and out, and I can hear the lewd sounds of the lube squelching in his hole.

Jay crawls over me to grab the lube and returns to his position behind me.

Boone doesn't try to reach out for me or participate at all. He's been told what his job is and he's a dutiful boy, preparing himself and nothing more until we direct him differently. Well, until Jay directs him differently. I'd let my sweet man do whatever the fuck he wanted, just to see the blissed-out look on his face. Luckily, what gives him that blissed-out look is Jay's urgent directions.

Cold slick hits my hole and I shiver. Boone's only reaction is a flaring of his nostrils as he takes a sharp inhale. I can imagine him picturing what Jay is doing to my hole right now.

I lean my head on my forearms, trying to relax and let Jay

open me up. It doesn't take much, but I love the thought of him playing with me, watching his own fingers slide and pry open my pucker until it's gaping for him.

His blunt tip nudges my opening and I gasp, a reflex that slowly eases as he rubs a hand along my lower back, stroking the top of my ass to relax my muscles. His hands are magic and I'm soon putty, slumping down into my arms and letting myself open around him and let him in.

"Beautiful," he murmurs as my hole swallows his cock. "So good. Cameron, it's like my dick was made to fit inside you."

The warmth from his words spreads and I melt a little more, falling into the spell of Jay's cock rocking into me, until movement from Boone grabs my attention. Three of his fingers split him open and his mouth hangs agape.

It takes me a moment to get my mouth wet enough to speak.

"Let me fuck him, Jay. I want to feel Boone around me while you fuck me into him."

Jay hums his approval and relaxes his hold on me. We shift together, sliding apart a little but not completely removing him from my body, until I'm farther onto the bed and situated between Boone's thighs. Jay hands me a condom and my hands shake, taking much longer than normal to get the fucker on. I'm so strung out, I'm even cursing mentally now. God, what these men do to me.

I press his knees against his chest until his bottom rises to the right angle for my cock. He breathes deep, his eyes closed and mouth open as I tease myself into him, inch by inch. With every inch forward, Jay's cock slides away, then back again as I ease off Boone. We go through the motions slowly until I bottom out, my trimmed pubic hair scraping against the sensitive skin of Boone's rim.

"I'm there," I groan and reach back to pat Jay's hip. "Fuck me. Hard. Force me into him as hard as you can."

Jay reels back and thrusts into me with as much force as he can, punching the breath from me and forcing a shout from Boone.

"Am I going to split you open, sweetheart?" Jay coos to Boone. "I'm going to fuck you so hard with Cameron's cock that you choke on his cum. You aren't going to be able to walk tomorrow, we're going to fuck you so good."

Jay continues his punishing thrusts, and I cling to Boone, unable to do anything but hold on for the ride.

My cock expands and throbs, more so when I feel his metal cock cage digging into my stomach. He can't get hard, but he's wet as his precum pools onto his belly, forced out by my cock from Jay's sharp thrusts.

My balls tighten and I shout that I'm going to spill. My vision goes white and all I can feel is the pounding in my head and my chest and my balls, and Jay's tight fingers digging into my sides.

Cold air on my back clears my head enough that I come to, realizing that I'm squishing Boone. His fingers scratch along the short hair at my scalp, comforting me as I return to myself. I lever myself off of him and he groans as he moves his thighs, flexing muscles that were stretched to the limit with our lovemaking.

I roll off him and he curls up into my side. I toss the condom into the trash can beside my bed and hear the flush of a toilet in the distance. The lamp flickers off and the bed shifts as Jay returns, curling around Boone from the other side. My breathing evens out as the thudding in my chest finally steadies.

With these two men around, I doubt it will remain that way for long.

20

JAY

I wake to the gentle rocking of Boone pressing his caged cock into the mattress. I'm not sure what time it is, but the room is still dark enough to think it's nowhere near morning yet. On his other side, Cameron still sleeps on his back with his arm thrown across the other pillows and his mouth hanging open with soft snores matching his deep breaths. They're both too adorable for words.

"You wouldn't be trying to get off, would you?" I whisper into Boone's shoulder and his body tenses. I press a kiss into that strong muscle, somehow made prettier for the freckles dotted across, even though he doesn't have them anywhere else that I've seen. "I think that calls for punishment, don't you?"

"Please," Boone whines so prettily.

I uncover us both and he shivers from the chill of the early morning air. The lube sits on the nightstand, and I reach inside for another condom.

"I haven't gotten to fuck this gorgeous ass yet. I think it's my turn this morning," I say, opening the cap on the lube and wetting my fingers. I spread the slick around his hole and he draws a sharp breath. "Are you sore?"

"No," he says, turning his head to face me. His arms pillow his head and he smothers a moan on his forearm as I press a finger into him. "It's just cold."

I pump my finger in and out slowly and reach between his legs with my other hand. His balls are full and heavy, and underneath I can feel wet along the cold metal of his cock cage.

"Have you been dripping all night?"

He nods into his arms as he rocks his body in time with my finger. I add more lube and another finger, and his hips thrust with even more urgency. Poor thing, trying to get hard when he can't.

"You were so good for us last night; should I let you out?"

"Please, Jay. I need it."

He whines when I remove my fingers but continues to hump the mattress while I feel around for the key. Cameron pocketed it last night, and his pants landed somewhere near my side of the bed. The wood floor is cold on my feet, but I find the pants and the key and then take a few seconds to enjoy watching Boone try his best to ease his suffering to no avail. It makes a smile spread across my face, knowing he loves the torture as much as I love giving it to him.

"Roll over." I pat at his thighs and he rolls to fill the space on the bed that I vacated. I crawl up between his legs and unlock the cage, setting it and the key carefully on the nightstand. Boone's cock fills immediately and he pulls a pillow over his face and moans.

"Show yourself to me."

Boone pulls his knees to his chest, and my chest flutters at his readiness to do anything I ask. I wish I could see him better, wish I could see his hole that's probably still stretched from earlier with Cameron, before I slide my own cock into it. Instead, I rip open the condom and roll it down, adding more lube while he waits, holding himself ready for me. I dribble some more lube onto his hole and spread it into his channel with my thumb, thrusting shallowly as I go along. He's still quite sloppy from our earlier fun, a thought which has me gripping at my base to calm down, but I don't want to make him raw or sore.

Boone's opening relaxes easily around me as I push my cock inside, then retracts and grips and pulls like a vise – a hot, silky vise that tightens the deeper I go. It feels so good that I let words of praise for Boone fall without regard to volume. All I know right now is that he needs to know how wonderful he is for me, how tight and good and right. He's done everything I asked and this dizzying grip is my reward, when he's the one who should be rewarded.

"What a lovely way to wake up," Cameron says with a voice still scratchy from sleep.

"You've had him both times. I thought it was only fair that I get a go at this ass," I say, leaning forward to accept the kiss that Cameron lovingly bestows on my lips. He next leans down and gives Boone a similar greeting, and Boone moans into his mouth.

The tent of the sheet still covering Cameron gives away his excitement, and I reluctantly pull out of Boone's body. Stretching over him, my slick, condom-covered cock slides against his as I capture his mouth once Cameron releases it. Boone grinds up from underneath me, chasing any kind of friction, and Cameron chuckles nearby.

"I think our needy boy needs some attention. Isn't that right, sweetness?"

"Yes. Please, fuck me. I don't care who. Just fuck me."

Cameron and I both laugh and I lean back, giving Boone room to rearrange.

"Hands and knees, baby. I've been wanting to try this ever since Cam came to me with the idea of a threesome."

Boone complies and I tease his presented hole with my cock,

sliding it along the slick that has dripped along his crack. Feels so good.

"You're going to suck Cameron while I fuck you so hard, you choke on his cock. Do you think you can come from that?"

"God, yes," Boone whines, and soon I hear the telltale sound of slurping and gagging and I know he's going down on Cameron's dick. I punch into him, loving the way the sounds get louder, the wet pop as he coughs before going right back at it. My cock-hungry slut. Correction, our cock-hungry slut.

Boone is the first to blow, not too surprising since he's been pent up all night. He shouts around Cameron's cock and I fuck him through it, enjoying the convulsing of his muscles around me, spurring me closer and closer to my own release. Cameron grips Boone's head and holds him close. The way his mouth hangs open and his eyes roll back tell me he's pouring himself down Boone's throat, and Boone relaxes around us both to take it. I slow my movements to keep him from gagging, but as soon as Cameron releases him, I return to thrusting with a vengeance. Each time I enter and graze Boone's overly sensitized prostate, he cries out, and I wish I could pull those sounds from him forever. But my release soon catches up with me, and with a final shove I pour myself into the condom deep inside Boone's body.

We collapse in a tangled heap, and I have enough presence of mind to dispose of the condom before letting sleep overtake me.

∽

I'M the first awake again, a hazard of my job. My internal clock won't let me stay in bed past six. Cameron still snores lightly away, while Boone is dead to the world. I think we wore the poor boy out. I ruffle through Cameron's drawers and find the sweatshirt that I now consider mine, then slip into the kitchen after a brief pit stop in the bathroom.

Cameron's cabinets are stocked with most of the basics, even though I know he doesn't do much cooking himself. It's enough to throw together some pancakes, and after a glance in the fridge, I decide to do a glazed cinnamon apple topping first. This is the first chance I've ever had to bake for someone I care about, two someones, and my heart sings with the opportunity.

The apples, sugar, and cinnamon heat in the pan, making the whole house smell delicious, while I whip together the ingredients for the pancakes and heat up Cam's skillet. I rummage through the drawers, looking for a spatula.

"Next drawer to your left," a scratchy voice says, making me jump.

I find the spatula and threaten Cameron with it.

"Those threats don't work with me." Cam grins and kisses my forehead before starting coffee. "Save it for Boone. I bet he'd love to have his bottom reddened with that thing. And I'd love to watch."

"Mmm, now I'm going to be hard while making breakfast. Thanks."

"How can you even think about going again? I'm worn out." Cameron leans over the coffee maker and inhales, like the scent alone is going to help revive him.

"Just remember how open you left yourself for that one and give me credit for not making an old man joke," I say, taunting him with the spatula one final time before actually starting in on the pancakes. Cameron takes a seat at his kitchen counter with his mug and watches me get to work.

"You're pretty when you cook. Actually, you're always pretty. The cooking is just an extra bonus for me."

I'd roll my eyes if I didn't need to watch the stove.

"I don't need the flattery. I'm already making you breakfast."

"Mmm," he moans as he inhales his coffee. "It's not flattery, it's the truth. Get used to hearing it, because I need to say it. It's important."

The apples simmer and the pancake bubbles perfectly around the edges before I flip it. As soon as a plate of three is stacked, I add some apples on top and slide it over to Cameron.

"God, this smells amazing," he says as he takes an exaggerated whiff. "Thank you, Jay."

"I hope you still think so after you taste them."

"Do you not have taste buds or something?" Cameron asks around a mouthful and a moan. "Is that why you have an overabundance of confidence everywhere except the kitchen?"

I try not to flush at the fact that he's noticed. Really, no one ever has before, but then no one has ever cared.

"It's because it's something I care about. I'm easily confident when it's something that doesn't really matter to me. But something I love and have worked hard at, like baking, it's harder to feign indifference. It's also why ..."

I take in Cameron's understanding eyes and patient features and my heart beats just a little faster. But no, I can't say it and make myself even more vulnerable. I've done enough of that already this morning.

"Why you aren't so cocky and flirty with us anymore? Because we mean something to you?" he asks in a gentle voice, like he's trying to soothe away my need to run away from this conversation.

A nod is all I can manage at the moment.

"You mean the world to us too, you know," Cameron says, rising from his kitchen stool and coming around to take my hand. The pancake is going to burn, but I don't care at the moment. "You should be feeling more confident in what we have here. Not less."

"Try telling that to my brain."

"Brain," Cameron whispers into the top of my head. "I am in love with Jay, so please stop worrying him."

The response lodges in my throat while Cameron wraps an arm around me and takes the spatula to dispose of the burnt pancake. He turns on the vent to clear out the smoky smell and drapes himself around my back, taking my hands in his before starting a new pancake.

"Let's take Boone's breakfast to him in bed, shall we?"

My stomach growls, but my heart is full, and I'd rather feed Boone than myself anyway.

"Make yourself a plate too," Cameron says. "I'll tuck you back in and feed you both."

I sink into his body a little more and feel myself losing a little more of my heart, but what a way to go.

21

BOONE

"I stopped by the dealership yesterday," my dad says over the phone, making me feel twelve years old again. "Would have been nice if I had known you quit your job beforehand, so I didn't look like an out-of-touch idiot."

Interesting that Buzz is claiming I quit and not that I was fired. Or maybe my dad is glossing it over in some weird lead-up to my own personal Big Bang.

"You never stopped by before, so I didn't think consulting you in my decision was necessary."

"More like, you didn't want to hear the truth about what a stupid decision it was. What were you thinking? Do you at least have something else lined up?"

"No, Dad. I'm trying to figure out what I want to do with my life."

"Well, let me bring you over a trash can, since you insist on throwing it away."

Why I answered the phone, I'll never know. He calls so rarely, and I never thought he'd find out about me getting fired. I planned on waiting to tell my parents until I had found a new job. At least it seems like Buzz didn't share why I had been fired, much less that it hadn't been voluntary like he had implied.

"Yes, of course," I say with a voice too tired to be amused. "Thanks for the pep talk. I feel all better now."

"Don't sass me. You need someone to whip some sense back into you. Maybe I should call Coach Anderson. He could always work the best out of you."

Sure, riding us until we were weak with exhaustion, demeaning us with insults all the while. Wonderful way to motivate, much less set an example for, teenage boys.

"Yep. That's what I need. A good whupping. Love you too, Dad."

I hang up before the temptation to share that I now have a wonderful place to get a good whupping, and it really is helping me discover who I want to be as an adult, becomes too much to hold back.

Instead of the usual hole in my chest after speaking to my dad, especially after hearing what a disappointment I am repeated in a million different ways, I have the urge to be with people who don't think I'm a loser. People who love, or at least like, me just the way I am.

Besides, talking with my dad gave me an idea. He'd be horrified at the way my mind is turning, and even more so to know that wanting to be the complete opposite of him and Coach Anderson in every possible way was the impetus for my decision. But it's time I follow my own dreams and stop being scared of them because of my father.

I pull up our group text and send out a message.

Boone: Do you think we can all get together this afternoon? Maybe at Jay's?

When no one answers right away, the nerves return, thrumming underneath my skin like creeping ivy until I give up and send another text out of desperation.

Only for Us

Boone: I'll bring the topic of conversation if Jay brings the muffins.

To my utter relief, two sets of three rolling dots appear onscreen.

Cameron: Can it be evening instead of afternoon? I'm not free until six.

Jay: I'm out of the muffin making business.

Cameron: No! Say it isn't so!

I gasp along with Cameron's text and type back.

Boone: But I never got to try any!

It's true and, given that I've heard Cameron go on about them for weeks now, totally unfair.

Jay: Don't make me punish you for being a brat.

Boone: Punishments. Hmm. Yet another thing like muffins that you claim to dole out, but I have yet to see any proof.

It's a good thing I don't have roommates, even if I'm probably going to have to find a cheaper place to live so I don't deplete all my savings, because right now I'm sure I look like a completely besotted fool with a mile-wide grin and flushing cheeks.

Jay: Someone's feeling feisty today!

Boone: I'm in a good mood, and I want muffins. Please?

Cameron: I'll bring dinner if Jay will make muffins. Boone, tell me what you want, since this is your evening.

I'm enjoying myself too much to hold it in. My smart-ass mood from earlier has morphed into something feisty, as Jay put it, and the thought of spending the evening with my two favorite men has me bouncing with excited flirtatiousness.

Boone: What goes well with muffins? Maybe that mix and match soup and pasta place?

Jay: Fine. But I choose the muffins and you are getting spanked later for being such a demanding brat.

My stomach flutters at the text, all hot and good, like how Jay spanking me would make me feel.

Cameron: Do I get to watch?
Boone: But I want all the flavors. Cameron got to taste all the flavors. Why can't I?
Jay: More spankings for you, mister.
Boone: Oh darn.
Cameron: Jay, I think you got played.

∽

MAYBE IT WASN'T RIGHT for me to suggest Jay's place instead of waiting for someone to volunteer. My space is too small and I only have a twin bed, so my apartment is out. I feel a little bad thinking it, but the last thing I wanted was Cameron's slick, cold apartment. I needed some loving, and Jay's home feels like a home.

Jay answers the door in cut-off jean shorts, bare feet that make my heartbeat speed up, and a crop top that reads, "Do you mind if I Slytherin?" The apartment already smells of warm spices, and I kick my shoes off by the front door after Jay releases me from a demanding hello kiss. All I'm missing is a cup of cocoa and a pair of fuzzy socks.

"Make yourself at home," Jay says, gesturing to his living room. "Cam isn't here ye–"

A knock on the door interrupts him, and seconds later Cameron enters with bags of food, bestowing kisses in a scene that feels domestic – and so sweet it makes my teeth hurt – in a way I never dreamed I'd actually crave.

"It smells delicious. Set up on the coffee table. But first, Boone, go put this on." Jay reaches for a small, recognizable box that I hadn't noticed sitting on the coffee table and hands it to me. "We have to see how well you take your punishment tonight before we decide if you get to come."

Cameron laughs. "Hey, don't say we. If it were up to me, I'd make Boone come and come and come. You're the sadistic bastard who likes to make him wait."

Jay's smile turns from teasing to evil as he leans over and nips at the top of my ear. "And he's the lovely who wants it."

I whimper without meaning to, but between the slight pain at my ear, the delicious humiliation of Cameron knowing what I like and laughing, and the heavy weight of the box in my hand, I'm about to shoot in my pants. Maybe the cage isn't such a bad idea.

When I get back, the food has been spread out across the coffee table.

"What would you like?" Cameron asks, and I'm about to argue that I can manage, I remember from the fond look in Cameron's eyes that he likes doing this part – the caring. I point to the different salads and ask for small samples of everything, as well as a big slice of the thick, fluffy bread. He pours a small amount of roasted red pepper soup into a mug and sets the plate onto my lap and the mug in my hand.

He'd make a great dad someday, I think, and then am shocked by the thought. I've never thought about kids, either in relation to myself or to my friends or lovers. Relationships, much less kids, seemed like such an impossibility that I never bothered. But here in Jay's loving home and with Cameron's gentle touch, I can only too easily imagine happy children running around.

You'd think those thoughts would have me softer than the cock cage, but they really don't. What the hell is happening to me? And why am I so damn happy about it?

"So, what is it that you wanted to tell us?" Jay asks, sitting on my other side on the couch. It's a little small for three people, especially with me sandwiched in the middle, but I really don't mind.

"I talked to my dad today," I say, and as the story pours out, looks of horror and anger and then a little pride cross their faces. One wouldn't even need to hear the story, just watch their expressions to get the gist of it. "But it made me realize something."

My plate's still full, but as I talk, I pick apart my bread for something to do with my hands.

"I wonder if I tied you up if you could focus better," Jay says out of nowhere and I choke on my own spit.

Cameron hands me a water. "Drink," he says and watches to make sure I don't choke again. When he's satisfied that I'm no longer on death's door, he picks up a shred of bread and holds it to my lips. "Eat."

I open at the command and taste his fingers along with the buttery crust.

"You aren't helping him focus, Cam," Jay says with fake annoyance. I know it's fake, because his eyes are smiling as he watches us.

"No, I'm feeding him. He can finish his story when he has food in his stomach."

I let Cameron take care of me for a few minutes more, but if I don't return to my story, I'm going to beg them for their cocks here and now. Cameron feeding me has left me with an intense desire for more things, bigger things, in my mouth.

"I think I know what I want to do," I say, and Cameron scoots back an inch to give me space to think and share.

"And?" Jay urges, not so giving.

"I want to get my teacher's license. I want to coach, but younger kids, where I can set a good example. Not like my own coaches or my dad."

Jay kisses my left temple and Cameron follows suit on my right. The care that they surround me with leaves me feeling jittery.

"I think it's a brilliant idea," Cameron says into my cheek.

"So good," Jay says. "You'll be a wonderful teacher. Thank you for sharing with us."

It seems like a ridiculous thing for him to say. I was excited to share it with them, but then yes, there was that little voice in the back of my head that sounds an awful lot like my dad, saying that teaching is for people who couldn't succeed at the subject. Teaching is for losers. That I'm not fit to be around kids, much less set an example for them. But the two sets of lips on my face fight that voice until all I can hear is "good" and "brilliant" and "wonderful."

"How can I punish you now that you've been so good for us?" Jay asks, and I whimper, worried that I'm not going to receive the punishments I worked so hard to earn.

"Please," I say in a stretched voice, and a puff of breath from Cameron warms my cheek.

"Take off your clothes," Jay orders and I scramble from the couch to comply.

Both men stay on opposite ends of the couch and watch as I strip my shirt first and then my jeans with trembling hands. I straighten before them in just my briefs, the cage obvious under the cotton, and shiver with the way their eyes caress my body. Jay raises an eyebrow and I drop my underwear, flaming with embarrassment at being seen in just a cock cage.

"Kneel between us and rest your upper body against the back of the couch," Jay says, and I fold my arms and bury my face into the knitted blanket draped across the sofa. The softness of it calms my nerves while I wait for the first blow.

"Now, why are you being punished, Boone?"

I struggle to remember as Jay drapes a hand along my lower back, rubbing in small circles, waiting for my answer.

"I was being a brat?"

Cameron chuckles to my left. I keep my face buried, but his

laughter makes my dick jolt against the cage. If I could get hard, I'd be like a diamond right now.

"Was that a question? Are you not sure? Or are you still being a brat?"

Jay's hand moves lower, caressing my ass, and I lose my breath. Softness and heat swirls in my head until Cameron's voice tickles my ear. "Breathe."

"Count for us, Cameron. Five spankings for being a brat, and five more for demanding every flavor of muffin."

Cameron's voice is low and gravelly in my ear, but I can't tell what he says as the sting of Jay's first spanking spreads across my right ass cheek. I bite my lip to keep from yelling at the shock. Jay swats the left cheek next, a matching sting, just as the right side begins to fade. Three and four pepper back and forth, until the stinging has faded into a spreading heat and ache.

My trapped cock throbs in the cage, dripping with pleasure from the torture I'm receiving. Cameron counts to five as Jay's palm hits the crease between my thighs and my ass, barely missing my balls. I can't hold back my groan at that, the idea of the humiliation and the pain if he hadn't missed.

Jay rubs a hand along my flaming skin, so sensitive that every stroke increases the ache. Even in my daze, I hear the snick of a cap and feel cold drip down my crack as a thick finger catches it and presses it against my hole.

"Please," I beg again, rubbing my face against the blanket like a cat. The finger presses against my entrance and I relax and let it in. So slick and so good. More precum drips and catches against the metal rungs of my cage.

The sixth smack shocks a gasp from my lips. Jay's palm landed to the side of the finger still exploring my ass, and I clench tight around it. Beside me, Cameron groans out a "Six."

Seven and eight don't hurt as much as they increase the sensation of the finger thrusting deeper inside me.

"Are you enjoying Cameron exploring your ass, sweetheart? As soon as I finish giving you the punishment you deserve, I'm going to add my fingers to your hole and you'll open up perfectly for both of us, won't you?"

I don't even remember the ninth and tenth spanking after Jay's words, but I can feel when his finger presses into me, and the two take turns twisting and teasing my passage with their fingers tangled together.

"Someday soon, we're going to both take you at once. Do you think we can train your hole to do that?" Jay asks, and Cameron and I both pant at his dirty words. In the distance, I hear zippers and the rustling of fabric. "You'd like that, wouldn't you? Having both of your men fuck you at the same time?"

"Yessss," I hiss, then gasp as wet heat streams across my back.

Jay gasps out his orgasm first, and I peek under my arm to watch him suck down Cameron's cock over my sticky, sweating backside. Jay's head bobs back and forth until Cameron taps his head. I can't look for long without my neck hurting, so I bury my face again and moan into my arms as another load lands across my back, mixing with Jay's.

My own cock drips onto Jay's couch, almost a steady stream now. The fingers return, prodding at my hole, although one hand reaches underneath to release the cage. With just a few more nudges against my prostate, I shout out their names as I paint the blanket and the couch underneath me.

Before the exhaustion of my orgasm takes hold, a giggle escapes my lips.

I got a good whupping indeed.

22

CAMERON

I knock on Boone's apartment door. I've picked him up here before, but he never seems to let me enter. I'm afraid my apartment left him feeling inferior, and I hate that. I tried calling first, but I have good news and I wanted to deliver it in person.

Boone peeks through a crack in the door and then opens it to his full width when he sees me.

"I have coffee and news," I say, holding up the tray of cups that are decorated with hearts. One cup is for "Sweetheart" and the other is for "Handsome." In my other hand, I have papers. "Jay was working so he sends his love. I think you're sweetheart."

Boone looks at the cups and smirks at me. "Don't worry. I think you're more than just a pretty face."

"You'd better." I bend and give him a quick kiss before entering his apartment. "Or I won't share the settlement offer that I just received earlier today from the Super Motors attorney."

In his surprise at hearing that we'd received an offer, Boone forgets to be worried about his apartment and plunks down on a small fold-out metal chair near a folding table. A quick glance shows it's the only table in his apartment, a place that looks more like a kid's dorm room than an adult's home. I take a seat on the other metal chair opposite him and set my briefcase on top. A sip of my coffee cup reveals that it's the Chai again. I mentioned to Jay that it was my favorite so far. Of course he remembered.

"Really? So soon? What is it? Is it good?"

I try not to smile at his barrage of questions. I'm sure I'd be overwhelmed too, in his shoes. It's one of the reasons that I wanted to deliver this news in person. That, and I'll take any excuse to be near Silas Boone.

"Take a drink of your coffee and relax. I've brought a copy to go over with you. We'll take this a step at a time."

Boone shifts in the seat, only then seeming to notice that I'm inside his apartment.

"I obviously don't have Jay's talent for decorating," he says as if it's an apology for the state of his place.

"I don't either. My place is as sterile as they come. I don't know how to decorate to save my life. If it weren't for my mom sending me some of my favorite old pillows from home, I wouldn't have a single personal thing in my place."

"Yeah, but yours looks like it could be on the cover of a magazine."

I sigh and stand, taking Boone's hand and walking him over to his faded leather couch. I make him sit and kneel at his feet, holding both hands firmly in mine.

"Do I seem like the kind of man who would let the state of a man's apartment change his feelings?"

Boone glances around at his apartment filled with second-hand furniture and little that shows who the man is. A football poster. A silver-framed photo of a woman I bet is his mother. His CSU diploma leans against the wall, crooked in its frame and covered in dust.

Only for Us

When he returns his eyes to me, he gives a small shake of his head.

"Do you know what I think?"

"What?" he says with a scratchy voice that breaks my heart.

"I think you and I both need to ask Jay for help. I think he would love it. And I know I'd love to have pieces of him in my place. Wouldn't you?"

Actually, what I'd like is to find a place for all three of us, but I know it's too soon. Somewhere that Jay can make a home. A safe harbor where Boone can study while he tries to earn his teaching license. A place for all of us to always be together.

"Yeah. That's a good idea. As long as he doesn't expect us to help." Finally, that serious and concerned face flashes a small smile, and I melt. "These aren't crafting hands."

His not-crafting hands are still held tightly in mine and I open them up to face his palms.

"Don't you dare insult these hands," I say, pressing a kiss to one palm and then the other. "They are incredibly talented. I may not have seen you in action back in the day, but I've read stories. And I have some personal experience with them too. I happen to be extremely fond of these hands, so back off."

Boone flushes with pleasure. "The offer?"

If my adorable man wants to deflect about the worthiness of his hands, so be it. I have good news to share. I grab my briefcase from the table and return with it, pulling out the copy of the offer I printed out less than an hour ago.

"They've offered two choices of settlement. The first is your job back, with back pay and compensation for any injury suffered during your unemployment. They'll also offer you a new demo car of your choice."

"The demo car is the only decent-sounding part of that offer. I miss my truck. My old Accord from college just isn't the same. And the second?"

I curb my smile, but I had guessed he wouldn't choose the first option. He has no desire to return to the dealership, especially now that he has a new idea and path forward for his life. One that I hope will make him very happy, and that I can imagine him fitting into for a long, enjoyable career.

"The second is back pay to date, plus an additional six months' compensation, and a glowing letter of reference from Buzz Superczynski, which is attached."

"Oh, I have to read that. Buzz has never said a good word about anyone in his life." I hand the letter to Boone, who scans the letter and laughs out loud. "Jesus Christ, that's the best thing I've ever read in my life. How it must have pained him to write it. That or he just had someone else do it and never set eyes on it himself."

I nod at the definite possibility. It certainly sounds like a lawyer, and not a car salesman, wrote it. Boone's smile is light and happy as he looks to me.

"What do you think? Should I accept door number two? I was never interested in getting my job back anyway."

I kiss his tanned nose and his joy-reddened cheeks and his bright smile, his eagerness rubbing off on me.

"As your boyfriend, I will support whatever you choose. But speaking as your lawyer, it is a good offer."

He rubs his nose against mine before leaning cheek against cheek with a sigh.

"It feels so good to be done with it. Thank you."

We support each other, letting the warmth seep from skin to skin, sharing air and comfort and enjoying the feeling of accomplishment and justice that so often doesn't come with my job.

"What time does Jay get off work?" Boone asks, still seeking the soothing presence of my touch.

"Not until nine. He's covering for Anna. Her kid is sick."

His stubble tickles my lips when I speak, but I don't move

until he does. He pulls back with a gleeful grin, and I can imagine him as a boy on Christmas morning.

"Let's surprise him with dinner. I want to celebrate."

"Sounds like a fantastic plan."

∽

WE INVADE the coffee shop five minutes before closing, and Jay sneaks us into the back while he closes up. When he hears the news, he gives Boone a kiss and a promise for reward that evening, and I have to insert myself just to make sure that we still make it out to dinner and not just back to Jay's place. Not that I'd mind, but I skipped lunch in order to bring Boone the news, and I'm starving.

When I suggest the same pub where Boone and I had our first date, a look of guilt flashes across his face.

"None of that, now," I say and put a firm arm around his waist. "We had fun, right? The rest doesn't matter. And besides, it will give us more opportunity to watch you bend over for us."

"I vote for that," Jay chimes in.

We order pizzas and rack up for a game of pool. With Jay egging him on, Boone loosens up in no time and begins teasing us both with suggestive stretching and bending. Jay responds with all sorts of suggestions for Boone's reward that has Boone scratching his shots.

Just as Jay leans across the table to give Boone a glimpse down his loose top that has Boone white-knuckling his cue, an unfortunately familiar voice shrills behind us.

"Boone, I've been hoping to run into you."

Boone's face turns green and he braces himself against the pool table. Jay rushes forward and places a hand against Boone's forehead.

"Babe, are you okay?"

Alison steps forward with a fluttering hand against her chest. "Oh, is this your boyfriend? I thought ... Well, never mind. I'm so glad to see you."

"I can't say the feeling's mutual."

Alison flinches at Boone's honest rebuttal, but forges ahead. "I've been wanting to tell you how sorry I am that you got fired."

"That you got me fired, you mean."

"I did not." Alison's forehead creases and her voice rises, but Boone keeps his back to her.

"Oh," Jay says, understanding dawning, and rubs a hand between Boone's shoulder blades. "This is the bitch that outed you at work?"

"I didn't know it was a secret," she says with her nose in the air. "I was just trying to help him find a match."

"He was doing just fine on his own." Boone doesn't need me to come to his rescue, but I can't keep quiet. This woman has done nothing but cause Boone distress, all because she's a nosy little priss. "In the future, maybe you could learn to mind your own business."

"Sure. If I hadn't butted in, he'd have never come out, and my poor friend Sonia would still be pining for him. I did him a favor."

"You did yourself a favor. You got him fired," I say, sweat starting to collect at the base of my neck.

Boone reaches over and rubs my back, which only serves to make me feel worse. I shouldn't be the one needing comforting right now.

"You obviously need to practice minding your own business," Boone says and follows it with a laugh. My beautiful strong man is laughing at Alison, when all I could manage was trying not to strangle her. I'm so not worthy. "Why don't you start now?"

Alison huffs away, and Boone collects the two of us in his arms.

"You're incredible. You know that, right?" I say to Boone.

"I draw strength from both of you," Boone says, kissing each of our lips in turn. "We're incredible together."

"I'll drink to that." Jay cheers and pinches my ass. By the way Boone jumps, I'm guessing he got a pinch too. "Now, whose turn is it? I'm ready to do some more ogling."

23

JAY

"Oh, thank God you're here," Kieran says the second I set foot into Armstrong House. "If I'm alone with Craig for one more minute, he might not make it to the ceremony."

"I can't imagine Craig as a groomzilla," I say and set down the first box of antique bottles with a rattle. "Come on, there are still two more of these to go."

"Anything to get away."

Poor Craig. We race past him as he's speaking with someone from the staff, and he really does look frazzled all to hell. Outside, it's the perfect day for a June wedding.

When we return from the waiting Uber with the rest of the bottles, Craig is nowhere to be seen.

"Thank God. Let's hurry before he can come back and change his mind about every fucking thing," Kieran says, pulling bottles out on one of the side tables that hasn't already been set for the reception. The place settings are a simple ivory and silver and our DIY décor goes perfectly.

"He can't be that bad," I say as I adjust some of the ribbons that have gotten pulled from the perfect bows I tied at home.

Kieran's hearty laugh lasts entirely too long to be real and ends with a pointed, and slightly crazed, look in my direction.

"I'll do the place cards. You do the centerpieces. Is Mal here yet? They're good at keeping Craig distracted."

"Haven't seen them."

"Damn," Kieran says and pulls out his phone and begins to text furiously.

If this is what Kieran is like for someone else's wedding, I think he's going to be the groomzilla for his own someday. His red hair sticks up to match the crazy look in his eyes. Whatever Mal texts back seems to relax him, because he puts his phone away and begins to work on the place cards.

Earlier this week, I went over to Kieran and Ted's house and spray-painted dozens of pinecones silver while Ted handwrote each place card in calligraphy. I thought Kieran was going to come in his pants as he discovered Ted's hidden talent and watched him carefully script each one. It was pretty and graceful, so I could see how Kieran might find it erotic. I didn't stay long. Fastest spray-painting job ever.

The Armstrong House let us keep the cut flowers for the centerpieces in their refrigerator overnight, so once I have the bottles placed in a very deliberate way to look as eclectic and effortless as possible, I return with the flowers and begin the most challenging task.

Every once in a while, I hear Kieran mutter across the room and look up to see him frowning at the seating chart and moving things around. I try to keep my head down, though, and work as quickly as I can, but hours pass before long and my stomach growls to let me know it.

"Hey, have you eaten?" I yell across the room to Kieran, pulling him from his list. His forehead wrinkles like he has to think about it for a minute. Poor guy. He's going to need a drink and a hot bubble bath when this is all done. And I bet Ted is going to think twice before proposing any time soon. Holy crap, the stress of it all.

At least once my part is over with the centerpieces, I can chill out and enjoy the ceremony with Boone by my side. I wish we were all three attending together, making our relationship public and official. It still doesn't feel totally real, like we're still hiding away, when what I really want is to shout my happiness from the rooftops.

"No, Ted was still asleep when I left this morning. I had planned to stop and grab something, but I forgot."

"I can run across to Sunshine Café. Get us some coffees and biscuits."

"I will love you forever. Here." Kieran reaches into his back pocket for his wallet but I wave him off.

"BRB," I shout cheerfully. Coffee and two seconds away from all the stress has me bouncing with excitement.

The Sunshine Café is just a jaunt across the street. It's in an older house in the same pretty downtown Victorian neighborhood area where Armstrong House resides – but on a definitely smaller scale. The café is quaint, so you'd think their food would be delicate and light. No, they serve some hardcore chicory coffee, the kind that my dad would say puts hair on your chest, and biscuits the size of saucers. I stroll up to the counter at the back and place an order for two of each to go.

The place is crowded, as usual on a Saturday morning, with couples squeezed in at the tiny front room tables and families filling in the larger tables in the adjoining room and spilling out onto the deck in the warm June sun. It's a perfect morning for it, if I weren't too busy to enjoy it. I stay near the counter, but step aside so others can place to-go orders or pay their bills.

Through the doorway, there's a beautiful family sitting at a round table. A man who looks similar to Cameron from behind sits with his back to me, but next to him, a little boy has his feet in the chair and squats to cover the man's closely cropped hair with his floral napkin. The boy pats his head and giggles, which only grow louder as the man tickles him. Across the table, a little girl begs for tickles too, while a woman tries to tug her back into her seat in vain. The perfect family. Something I had never realized I wanted until that moment.

"Order for Jay," a voice from behind the counter calls out. I'm still mesmerized by the family, but the announcement startles the man into turning around. Familiar dark brown eyes meet mine.

"Order for Jay?"

The voice is closer, and I tear my eyes away from Cameron to take the bag and coffee carrier away from the server holding it out to me.

"Excuse me," I repeat over and over, pushing through the crowd to get out the door. Why is it suddenly so busy? The room closes in on me and I struggle to make it to the door. Fresh air fills my lungs and I run. Coffee splashes, but I don't care. My only concern is getting across the street and into the reception hall and hiding away.

"Whoa, what happened?" Kieran approaches when I enter the room. I can feel my eyes are wild and my heart is racing, but I can't stop it.

"Here," I say and thrust the food and coffee at him. "I have to go."

"Sit," he says and pulls out a chair for me. "You need to eat something. You look like you've just seen a ghost."

I can't even begin to process what I've just seen. I pinch off a bite of the biscuit that Kieran has opened and laid in my lap.

"Good," he says and urges me to take a sip of coffee. "Eat another bite. Now, what happened?"

"What was the conference that Cameron was going to this weekend?"

Only for Us

I should feel guilty using Kieran's work knowledge against Cameron, but after what I just saw, I have no guilt whatsoever. I can feel my phone vibrate in my pocket, probably some pathetic attempt at an explanation from Cameron.

"Conference? What?" Kieran kneels and puts his hands on my knees to stop them from shaking. "Why are you asking about Cameron?"

"I just saw him."

Kieran's eyes light up. "At Sunshine? Was he with Celeste? I've been dying to meet her."

"Who's Celeste?" My voice shakes but Kieran doesn't seem to notice. He's too excited about this Celeste person. Of course, he has no idea what all this is doing to me. We haven't talked about Cameron. As far as he knows, Cameron is only dating Boone. But what is obviously a casual conversation to him is tearing up my insides.

I want to believe in Cameron and everything he has said to me and Boone, but fuck. It was the perfect family. Right there, in front of my eyes. Cameron lied about where he was. What else has he lied about? I feel like I'm on one of those carnival rides where they spin you around and the bottom drops out. Only I have no guarantee it will come back together, at least before I puke my guts out.

"Celeste is Cameron's sister. She's from California. She and her family are here for a week visiting. He's been so excited. His mom and his sister have been bugging him to move back, and he wanted them to come here instead, so they could see how well he's doing. Did it look like they were having fun?"

My feet, they're solid on the ground, though I wiggle my toes to double-check. But dammit, I'm still on the verge of puking, either from relief that he doesn't have a secret family or distress that he still lied. Maybe both.

Why would he lie about his sister? Obviously so he didn't

have to introduce us, but that makes no sense to me. He said his family knows that he's gay. So why hide us? Unless he's ashamed that we're an us? My phone vibrates again, and I pull it out long enough to turn the fucking thing off and stuff it back into my pants.

Too many thoughts and feelings are whirling around in my brain and chest and stomach. I need Boone. I need him to ground me and make me feel normal again.

"I have to go. I have to get ready and pick up Boone. You've got everything under control."

"Yeah, sure. Thanks again for all your help. You're the best."

I try to force a smile at that, but I doubt I manage it. I might be the best, but I'm obviously not good enough.

24

BOONE

The beauty of the gardens of the Armstrong House in full bloom in June is lost on me. What I'm sure must be joy and utter devotion on display as the two grooms take their vows is also a complete blur. All I can think about is the man sitting in the row behind me, and the burning stare that threatens to set my collar on fire.

Jay once asked me if I had ever apologized to Arthur. At the time, he refused to take my calls or see me. Over time, I gave up, and figured it was for the best that I never tried to explain or at least say I was sorry. But now that I'm face-to-face, or heated neck to furious glare, I can't back down. I'm going to have to find a way to make him hear my apologies.

My seat feels too cramped and my legs uneasy. I'm surprised Jay hasn't smacked my jiggling legs and threatened to tie me up if I can't be still, but he seems to be in his own little world today too. I know he misses Cameron, but there's a sadness in his eyes that's been there since I picked him up. No amount of cajoling or misbehaving has pulled him from his funk.

A shot of joyful music fills the air like a burst confetti balloon, and as the grooms make their way down the aisle, kissing and hugging and waving at friends, I realize I missed the entire wedding worrying about the man beside me and the man behind me.

Before he can escape, I turn around and reach out a hand that a short "grrr" has me quickly retracting.

I think his date just growled at me.

"Arthur."

His pale blue suit looks like the height of style, highlighted by a pink floral bow tie. Just the same as I remember, but also not. Where once he was reserved and timid in his dominance, now he wears it like a glove.

"Silas," he says harshly, his eyes not blinking and his face as hard as stone. If I thought time might have softened his attitude toward me, I was wrong.

"Are you staying for the reception? I was hoping for a chance to talk to you."

"I don't think there's anything for you to say to him that either of us want to hear," says his companion, a shorter man, cute but feisty and looking for all the world at me like he'd like to take a bite out of my jugular if Arthur would let him off his leash long enough to do so.

But Arthur's hand calmly rests on his date's shoulder and he nods.

"That would be fine. I have a minute now, if you'd like? How are you, Jay? It's nice to see you."

At his name, Jay snaps out of his daze and takes in the couple that I've been talking to. "Dave. Arthur. It was a lovely wedding, wasn't it?"

Arthur leans down and whispers something in Dave's ear. Narrow eyes focus on me, but he nods and inches toward Jay, signaling his acquiescence to my speaking with his man.

We edge away from the gazebo where wedding pictures are happening and from the line of people trying to make their way inside to the reception. There's a garden bench by a bed of native flowers and Arthur leads me to it.

He sits and signals for me to follow.

"Huh. I guess I've always had a thing for take-charge guys."

Arthur raises his eyebrows at me, not in surprise, but like I'd dare to say such a thing.

"Sorry. I'm already screwing this up. Please. I'd like to apologize."

Arthur sits tall with his legs crossed, his hands folded in his lap. He's such a big guy, yet he manages to come across graceful and not fumbling. When he doesn't say anything, I take it as a sign to continue.

"There's no excuse for what I did. I was a cowardly kid who turned into a cowardly adult. In so many ways." I wish Jay were here to keep me strong and on track. I wish Cameron were here to rub my back and tell me how well I was doing. But I have to do this on my own. "I should have broken up with you the second I realized I was never going to get past my insecurities when it came to us. I'm sure you already realized all this a long time ago, but it wasn't you. You were wonderful. You were enough. It was me that was intimidated by your intelligence and how put together you were. It was me that wasn't strong enough to tell you what I wanted or needed."

Arthur glances at me, questions swimming behind his eyes, but he only says, "I hope you've dealt with those issues now, or I feel for any man you've dated since."

"I didn't date, at least until now. I was so worried, and I didn't want to be that cruel ever again." He flinches at the word cruel but doesn't say anything. "Arthur, I want you to know how sorry I am, for everything. You didn't deserve to be treated that way. I don't know if you can ever forgive me, but I wanted you to know that I'm so sorry for what I did, and so sorry that it happened to you."

That startles him, and he turns to me. "Was there someone else it would have been acceptable to screw over?"

"Oh, definitely. My father. If I had just stood up to him, told him to piss off with his masculine bullshit, then maybe I would have had the confidence earlier to be myself. Then no one but him would have gotten hurt."

Arthur does crack a smile at that. His first since I approached him. "Well, I'm usually not one to say I told you so, but I do remember saying a few things to you about your father's toxic masculinity."

"Yeah, unfortunately, you being right at the time only had the side effect of making me feel even less worthy of your attentions. It's a vicious cycle, one I'm sorry you got caught in."

Arthur's gaze softens. "But you're doing better now?"

"I'm great." My insides relax at just the thought of my two men.

"I'm glad." Arthur picks himself up and brushes off the seat of his pants. "I hope you enjoy the rest of your evening."

I stare as he walks away, wondering if he'll ever forgive me. Will I always be the asshole in his storyline?

25

JAY

Sitting around one of the side tables at the reception, my eyes focus on the petals of one of the white snapdragons. The entire afternoon blew by in a haze. I haven't said a word about seeing Cameron to Boone yet, and the internal debate over how to broach the subject and when is causing an ulcer. Right now, I have to focus on the practical. If I think about what it means for us, for our future, I'll break down, and that's the last thing I want people to see.

Ben stands from his seat on Zach's other side, his position as Zach's best man, and taps his champagne glass. After the rooms quiets down, he sets down his glass and begins to sign as he speaks. He's handsome in a tux, but my eyes catch on his hands. I'm not sure what he says – I can't bring myself to hear words about love and happiness right now – but the gracefulness of his hands as they sign his words surprise me. Ben and I were never going to be a thing, not really. It was probably obvious to everyone but me from the very beginning. But Ben now, not changed but made more sure by Jonathan's love, is a sight to behold.

I risk a glance at Boone, only to find him watching me and not the wedding party.

"What's the matter?" He leans over and whispers in my ear. "You haven't been yourself all afternoon. You didn't even threaten to spank me when I fidgeted during the ceremony."

Had he fidgeted? I can't believe I didn't notice.

"And why were you fidgeting like a naughty boy, anyway?"

I hope he doesn't notice the effort it takes to tease him. I want to be as good for him as he is for me, even if my heart isn't in it at the moment.

"Seeing Arthur again, for one."

"Right. How did that go?"

Apologizing to Arthur was a big deal for Boone. I need to get my head out of my ass and support him.

"Good, I think. I doubt he'll ever forgive me, but at least I got to say I was sorry. I think he knows I mean it. Wholeheartedly."

"How could you not?" I lean over and nuzzle his cheek and kiss the corner of his lips where a sigh escapes. "One mistake does not a man make. And you, my dear Boone, are a wonderful man."

He sighs again, and this time I do notice him fidgeting in his seat.

"I might have also prepared myself for you. Cage and all. Just in case weddings make you horny."

I stare up into Boone's sweet and loving eyes. There's no teasing; only a desire to please. How can I hurt him with the knowledge that I've been sitting on? Disappointing Boone would kill me.

"I love you."

The words slip through my lips like the most natural and true words ever spoken. As easily as ordering chicken for dinner or choosing coffee over tea. Still, Boone's eyes flare with surprise, and I realize I haven't done a good enough job showing or telling him before now if it comes as such a shock. He blinks rapidly and turns back to the toast now being given by Kieran.

I watch his back straighten, then slump, then straighten again. From my angle, I can't see his face unless he turns to me, but I can imagine the emotions raging across them. Finally, he puts me out of my misery and turns back to face me. His eyes are glassy with unshed tears, but he blinks them back with determination.

"I love you, too," he says, too loud to be a whisper, but I don't care if the entire table hears him. I don't care if his staunch declaration overshadows this entire wedding. Right now, it's everything I need.

"Let's get out of here," I lean forward and whisper into his ear. I don't care if we miss the cake or anything else. I need Boone to ease my aching heart.

Boone nods and we slip out a side door. His hand finds mine, and we walk intertwined through the parking lot to Boone's car.

"Really though," he says before opening the passenger door for me. "What's bothering you? I can help."

I hesitate, the words lodging in my throat.

"Communication, remember? Please."

His gentle voice and loving eyes ease the ache in my throat, and I breathe shakily.

"I saw Cameron this morning. His sister and her family are visiting."

Boone lets my words sink in, his face remaining neutral at first, and then scrunching in confusion. "I thought he was at a convention?"

I nod. "I asked Kieran about it, but he didn't know anything about a convention. Apparently, this visit with his sister has been in the works for a while. He used the convention as an excuse so he didn't have to tell us his family was in town."

Boone's hand still holds mine, and now he lifts it to his chest, sandwiching it between his beating heart and warm hands.

"You're rushing to conclusions. I know. I'm tempted to do the same."

I open my mouth to argue, but Boone stops me with a kiss. It's simple and chaste, but for the first time, Boone is putting me in my place instead of the other way around.

"He shouldn't have lied," Boone finally says against my lips when we part for breath. "But concocting wild notions and letting our imaginations run away is not helpful. Tonight, you're going to focus on me. I've never had anyone tell me that they love me before, and I want to relish it. You're going to make love to me, and tell me you love me over and over again. And I'll tell you the same thing."

My hands tremble inside his. I don't know how to react with Boone taking charge like this. It makes me feel … wanted.

"Then tomorrow, you and I will go over to Cameron's place and we will talk about this like rational adults in a relationship. We will let him explain," he says, and when I hiccup as I open my mouth to argue, he adds, "And we will let him know how much he has hurt us both. Because communication goes both ways."

I'm too overwhelmed to do anything but bury my face against his chest and hope he doesn't mind the tears soaking into his dress shirt. Boone's large hand strokes my hair and neck, and he whispers soft words against my temple.

"Tonight, forget about everything but you and me and how much we love each other."

My body shudders under his touch, and I try to click my brain off and only feel Boone here with me. Boone, who loves me. Boone, who's going to take care of me tonight.

26

CAMERON

The remainder of that Saturday is excruciating torture. After Jay fled from the Sunshine Café, I tried to text and call him, but got no response. I did, however, get a world of response from my sister.

She pummeled me with question after question – "Who was that?" "Why did he look so shocked?" "What's going on?" – until I finally had to admit that Jay was someone I was dating.

Unfortunately, that only led to more questions.

By the time Matthew, Celeste's husband, caught up with us after his hike, she was about to burst with curiosity. I wasn't about to share my love life in front of the kids, in case there was a bad reaction from their mom. It was safest to do it when Matthew could take them elsewhere, so we split up. Matthew took the kids to a movie, despite Celeste wanting to keep them away from screens, much to their delight. And I took Celeste to Espresso Patronum.

Now that we're at the table, Celeste with tea in hand and looking expectantly at me while I ignore her in favor of my plain coffee, I regret this decision. We should have gone to a bar. I need some liquid courage right about now.

"You're dating again, Cammy. That's good," she says in her supportive big sister voice. I know them all. There's disapproving, judging, know-it-all, and on-the-verge-of-throttling. She's mostly outgrown those last two. "Did you think I wouldn't approve of you dating again? Or did you think I wouldn't approve of him?"

"It's not that," I say with a sigh. I've tried to figure out how to say this for weeks, and nothing sounds right in my head. If I had selected a best option, it's flown out of my head now. "I'm in a relationship with two men."

"Do they know about each other?"

"Not like that. We're all in a relationship together."

"A throuple?"

"God, I hate that word."

I rest my forehead on the palm of my hand, waiting for the sermon to begin. Dreading it, really. Instead, a whoop and a cheer erupt from the other side of the table, and I peek through my fingers.

"Ha ha! Go Cammy!"

Out of all the reactions I anticipated and prepared counter-arguments for, this was not among them.

"Who are you and what have you done with my sister?"

Celeste frowns at that and reaches across to pull my hand away. "Did you really think I would judge you? Cammy, you've been so laser-focused and serious your whole life. Dylan helped. He brought out a playful side in you, although I debate whether he was doing it for himself or for you. Regardless, I loved Dylan and I was happy that he made you happy. You deserve a chance to finally live it up and have some fun."

"But we are serious, Cel. I'm in love with both of them."

She studies me for a minute before a wicked grin breaks out. "Mom's going to flip."

Now there's a reaction I anticipated.

"Please let me tell her. Not you."

"At least let me be there."

"No."

"I'll support you. Defend you. You need me." She tugs on my hand like I'm keeping her from admittance to the best show all year. Actually, that's probably fact and not an analogy. Either way, when I do finally tell my mom, it's going to be private viewing only. No audience.

"Nope. Not going to happen."

Celeste sighs and flops back in her chair.

"Two, huh? Tell me about them."

For the next hour, I tell her every wonderful, unique, beautiful, and maddening feature of each of my men, and then proceed to explain how I fucked up.

"Surely they can understand you wanting to tell me by yourself. Suddenly being faced with the three of you together, I might have been a little more ..."

"Surprised?"

"Blunt." Celeste laughs and slaps her thigh. "Oh my God, the things my children are going to learn."

"You don't have to tell them," I say, but squirm in my seat at the thought of hiding our relationship. It's one thing not to be ready to tell people and take your time. It's another to actively hide it and lie. "If you don't think it's appropriate."

"Cammy, you really are something. If those two men feel anything close to what you obviously feel for them, you should be proud to share that with the world. My kids can deal. I can deal. The world can deal. I just hope I don't have to explain DPs or anything like that. But you never know. They ask some crazy questions."

Her mouth twists as she obviously remembers some previously uncomfortable conversations. After spending the week with the two of them, I'm not surprised. They definitely take after their mother, and blurt out the most random, and sometimes shocking, things. It's a fun age to be their uncle, but I doubt being the parent is quite as amusing.

"Fight for them. I know you think they are better off without you, but believe me. You make every life you touch better."

The only problem is, I'm at a loss as to how to fight for them.

When I get home from dropping her off at their hotel, I waver on how to proceed. Try to call again? It looks like Jay has blocked me. I could just show up to his house, but what if that makes him angrier?

I've refrained from reaching out to Boone, because I don't want him to feel like he has to be the intermediary in this relationship. We stressed communication was key, and the breaking of that trust was my fault alone. It's up to me to be the adult and try my best to repair the damage that I've caused, and if I can't, accept it.

As I stare helplessly at my phone, it dings with an incoming text. Unfortunately, not from any party I've been hoping for.

Kieran: Hey. How is Celeste liking Fort Collins?

Cameron: Fine.

Kieran: Uh-oh. Just fine? Are they going to keep pestering you to move back to Cali, do you think?

Cameron: She loves it. Having a great time. But I messed up.

Kieran: Your sister loves you. I'm sure she'll forgive whatever it was.

Cameron: Not my sister. I need some advice.

Kieran: Come over for dinner? Ted's making stir-fry.

Cameron: That would be great. Thanks.

My relationship with Ted has always been a little odd. Ted was Dylan's first, and in my opinion true, love. As soon as I met him in person, I understood. Ted's the sort of solid, stand-up kind of guy I always wished I could be. He helped me get through Dylan's death, took me in to his home when I couldn't face California any longer, and helped me start a new life in Fort Collins. I'm not the best of friends with their little group, Ted and Kieran excepted, but Ted is certainly the backbone, the anchor that keeps them all together.

"Are they still here? Does she really like Fort Collins?" Kieran asks the second I set foot in their house. "Then again, how could she not? You could have brought them for dinner, you know."

"Nah, I didn't want to bother you. And I think she's ready for a night away from me and my misery."

"And what misery is that?" Kieran asks as he ushers me through the dining room and into the kitchen, where Ted mans a giant wok. A skillet on a nearby burner bubbles with oil, and Kieran encourages me to help.

"It's fun. Like playing with Play-Doh," he insists despite my skeptical look.

Kieran hands me small balls of dough to roll out, then I hand the flattened dough back and he tosses them into the skillet. The sizzling sounds and the delicious smells fill their kitchen and make me long for Jay.

"Where all have you taken your sister and her family?" Ted asks over his shoulder as he keeps his attention on the wok.

"We went to Rocky Mountain National Park and did some shopping up in Estes Park. Touristy stuff mostly, but I think they're having a good time. They love the weather."

"Be glad they visited in June and not August, or they might not have been as impressed," Ted says, and I agree.

"Well," Kieran says. "We missed you at the wedding. It was beautiful."

He quirks a brow at me the way he does at work, the look that lets me know he's caught another one of my boneheaded mistakes and he's thoroughly pleased with himself.

"Jay especially."

"Jay was especially beautiful, or Jay especially missed him?" Ted jokes and Kieran swats him on the butt with a kitchen towel in retaliation.

"Both," he says haughtily, refusing to take Ted's bait.

"Did Jay say anything?"

I'm a coward for asking friends and not the source, but right now, I want to hear anything I can about Jay and how he was the rest of Saturday. Was he as much of a wreck as me? More? Did I completely lose my chance with him and Boone?

Kieran shrugs, like anything to do with Jay isn't a big deal, but the way he watches me like a hawk tells me otherwise.

"He seemed surprised to see you at the Sunshine Café. And even more surprised that I knew nothing about a work convention you were supposedly at this weekend. Does this have something do you with your miserable messing up?"

I take my time with the last piece of dough until finally Kieran lays a hand on the rolling pin, stilling my fidgeting.

"Whatever it is," Kieran says, "We aren't going to judge you."

Ted empties the wok into a bowl and turns to face me.

"I like to dance around in pleather harnesses." He says it with a laugh, but his arms are crossed in a defensive position and I know he's serious. "I'm hardly one to judge a lifestyle."

Kieran's face flushes like a tomato as he eyes Ted like he's imagining him prancing in pleather right then.

I appreciate the attempt at solidarity, but that's so much more of a mental image than I wanted of the two of them.

"Boone and Jay and I are together. Well, we were together before I screwed up yesterday. Now I'm not so sure."

Kieran picks up the plate of fried bread and we move to the dining room. He's still a little pink when he says, "I have to admit, I kind of guessed it."

"You did?"

My mind races back to anything I could have said, but there's nothing.

"Yeah. It wasn't so much in what you said, but in the way any of you three looked at the others. It was a little, um, intense."

Intense doesn't even begin to describe it. And now I've potentially lost it forever.

"Hey," Kieran says and shakes my arm to pull me out of my funk. "None of that. You three belong together. I don't think one little screw-up is going to ruin everything you've got. You just need a plan."

"A plan?"

"Oh Lord," Ted says, and picks up his fork, ignoring the daggers that Kieran shoots him.

"I am very good at 'I screwed up and I want to win you back' plans, thank you. Just look at Zach and Craig. All my handiwork," Kieran says, sitting tall in his chair. Ted coughs and raises his eyebrows, and Kieran deflates. "Fine. Not all me. Tell me, Cameron. Have you ever met Mrs. Hill?"

27

BOONE

When my alarm rings on Monday morning, Jay is still wrapped around me, just like he's been all weekend. I haven't given up on Cameron. I can't. My heart won't let me. But Jay seems to have lost all hope. We made love all through the night, Saturday and Sunday, and spent the day Sunday in each other's arms. I loved being there for him, but no matter how hard I tried to encourage or distract him, there was a Cameron-sized hole the entire day.

Jay talked more about what he saw and how much it hurt. I suppose that being in the closet for so long has its advantages. And honestly, if Jay were thinking rationally, he would also understand that this is similar to coming out. I'd hardly expect either one of them to spring it on their families.

As for mine, I finally went home last weekend and told them – both about deciding to become a middle school coach and about being gay and in a relationship with two men. I think my mom could have handled the coach thing; her eyes lit up when I mentioned it first. But the second I told them about how much I loved the two men in my life, my dad told me to leave and never come back. I can't say it didn't hurt, but being able to dismiss my father with a "Gladly" and a "Fuck you" eased a weight off my chest I never even knew was there. I kissed my mom and told her I'd be happy for her to contact me if she ever wanted. I think someday, she might get the guts to defy my father and reach out. One can always hope.

The more Jay and I talked last night, the more we decided that we needed to set aside a time to meet Cameron on neutral territory. It worked for me before, so once we're dressed and ready, we're driving to Cameron's office. I have no idea if he'll be in or have time for us, but if his family is still here, I'd hate to show up on his doorstep and force a conversation that he isn't ready for with them.

For once, Jay isn't awake before dawn and already sucking down caffeine, so I try to let him sleep a little longer and put on a pot of coffee while I take a shower.

"You should have woken me," Jay says, entering the bathroom as I'm exiting the shower. Normally I'd receive a suggestive look or comment about losing the towel. This morning, Jay steps to the toilet to pee and stares blankly at his dark and puffy eyes in the mirror like he isn't really seeing anything.

"I thought you needed more sleep," I say, pressing a kiss to his cheek and getting his t-shirt sleeve damp from my still-dripping torso.

"Is that your way of telling me I look bad?"

"It's my way of telling you I love you, and that I want you to feel better."

Jay huffs at the mirror. "It's going to take more than sleep," he mutters under his breath.

"Get ready. I'll make some breakfast, and then we can head out. I hope frozen French toast is okay. I don't have your talent for cooking."

"It's fine." Jay blinks and meets my eyes for the first time this morning. He tries to offer me a smile, and although it doesn't even reach his upper lip, much less his eyes, I'll take it. I'll take anything he can give me.

"Do you think we should call first?" Jay asks as we sit down at my metal card table for breakfast.

"I think he's going to be relieved to see us, which is what you're really asking, so no." I stab at the too-thin and grossly flimsy toast – Jay really has spoiled me at this point – and force it down with a gulp of coffee. "Hurry up. The sooner we get going, the sooner all of this will be behind us."

"How can you have such hope?" Jay asks. His eyelids droop and wet hair flops over a darkly shadowed eye before I push it behind his dainty ears with my syrup-sticky fingers. It's a testament to his mood that Jay doesn't protest.

"Because I never expected this to be easy. And I never expected it to feel so damn *right*."

We get to Cameron's office shortly after ten, and Kieran greets us each with a hug.

"We've come to talk to Cameron if he's available," I say. I probably sound strangely formal, but we are in a law office, after all.

"Oh, I bet you have," Kieran says with a knowing grin. Jay jolts and I steady him with an arm around his waist. "I've already suffered an entire evening, listening to him curse his own stupidity, so I was more than ready to pass the baton to someone else. You'll find him at his apartment."

"Should we go there? Is his family still here?" I ask as Jay's arm snakes around my waist and tightens. Thank God I have him to lean on through this. We can lean on each other. I'd be a raving mess if I was dealing with this on my own.

"Oh, you should definitely go there."

I nod my thanks and guide Jay to the door.

"Tell him I said good luck!" Kieran calls after us. I guess our threesome isn't such a secret anymore, at least among their group of friends.

Jay withdraws at Cameron's front door, but I clasp his hand in mine and pull him to my side. Cameron answers the door wearing a pink apron with brown polka dots, but he's covered from head to toe in flour.

Cameron's eyes light with hope when he sees us. He tempers his voice, but I can still hear it shake when he says, "Jay. Boone. I'm so glad you're here."

We follow him inside, and I'm surprised to find he's not alone. An elderly woman, old enough to be his grandmother but clearly not, shuffles around his kitchen with baking sheets in hand, while a female version of Cameron takes them from her and sets them on the counter. In the background, there are kids bouncing and singing to cartoons in front of the television, while a man on the couch shushes them.

"This tray is done, Cameron," the elderly woman says, leaning down and peeking into the oven. "Come see. The edges have lifted from the sheet and just started to turn golden. If they stay in the oven any longer, they'll be hard as brick bats to eat."

Cameron rushes to help her, and once her hands are free, she seems to notice the new additions to the apartment. I've never seen Cameron's place so chaotic, so it's no wonder no one noticed us.

"Ah, are these your men, Cameron? Introduce me."

That gets the other woman's attention, and she whips around to stare.

"Yes, ma'am," Cameron says, and gestures us into the kitchen. "Mrs. Hill, this is Jay Howard and Silas Boone." He then points to the woman watching us with interest. "And this is my sister Celeste."

Jay holds out a hand, but Mrs. Hill steps forward and throws her arms around his shoulders, then does the same to me.

"It's lovely to meet you boys. You have a good one here." She turns to Cameron and pats his cheek. "A little foolish, maybe. But he's got a good heart. You're the one that can actually cook, I think?" she asks as she looks back at Jay.

His eyes blink in surprise, and I answer for him, since he seems too shocked to speak.

"Yes, Jay's a wonderful baker."

She smiles at me and pats my hand. Her skin is as thin and soft as paper.

"I hope our creation meets standards. Just remember, they're made with love."

Celeste steps forward while Mrs. Hill takes off her apron and shakes it free of flour before folding it neatly and fitting it into a wicker bag. Cameron is distracted as she rattles off a series of instructions that he hastily copies down, and Celeste takes full advantage.

"It's ni–" Two arms stop me from finishing as Celeste pulls me in for a hug even tighter than the one from Mrs. Hill. Her chest stutters and I feel her shaky breath against my neck. It figures Cameron's sister would be almost as tall as me. She whimpers, then after one final squeeze, she moves to give Jay the same treatment. His eyes are wide with questions and I raise my shoulders, because I don't have the answers.

"Thank you," she says, blinking like she doesn't have tears clinging to her eyelashes. "Thank you both. You have no idea what it means to me to see Cameron happy again."

She calls to her family, and in a blur of commotion, all of them and Mrs. Hill are herded out the door. Celeste lingers long enough to say, "Hopefully, we can get together later, and you can meet everyone properly. But I know you have things to discuss."

"Goodbye, bird. Goodbye, sweetness," Mrs. Hill calls from the hallway. "Good luck. I'm rooting for you."

Jay still blinks in shock as he stares at the door closing behind her.

"What–"

He doesn't get any further before a strong arm and a hard chest cut him off. Cameron's other arm beckons me closer, and I join in.

"Oh God, I'm half afraid this is the last time I'll get to hold you both like this. I don't want to let go," Cameron says in a wavering voice.

"If you want me to breathe," comes Jay's muffled voice and Cameron lets go. Jay steps back with flour on the tip of his nose and smeared across his forehead. "We need to talk."

In that moment, I know everything is going to be okay. Jay clearly can't keep his voice as stern as he wants after that floury bear hug. He's already forgiven Cameron, whether he realizes it or not.

"I'm so sorry for lying to you both," Cameron says as we follow him into the living room. Flour puffs out from his apron as he sits and blends into the white leather. It's so funny looking, I have to bite my lip to keep from smiling. This is not the time, with Cameron so distressed and unsure. "I was scared. I knew it was the wrong choice as soon as I made it, but I kept going."

"Why did you lie?" I ask when Jay says nothing. He sits next to Cameron, and I see Cameron's chest inflate with hope, but Jay doesn't look his way. "It's not like we wouldn't understand you needing to take your time explaining this to your family. We would have given you space."

"That's the ridiculous thing," Cameron says as he flails his arms into the air, stirring more flour about. I resist the urge to undo his apron and save his living room, but it's hard. "I know that. I'm not ashamed or embarrassed by either of you or our relationship. But when it came down to it, my instinct was to hide and to lie."

Can't say I don't understand that instinct. I move until I'm in front of Cameron and kneel down to kiss his forehead. His eyes well with tears and he closes his eyes, though it doesn't hide his pain.

"And that's what upsets me," I say, leaving my forehead resting against his, sealing the kiss into his skin.

Jay leans forward and rests a hand on Cameron's knee. The shudder of emotion that overtakes Cameron's body at our tender ministrations is almost enough for me to end this now and drag both of my men to bed. No more talking. Forgive and forget and love. That's what I want, even though what we need is to get all this out in the open so we really can move forward.

"You lied," Jay whispers, finally finding his broken voice. "You go on and on about how this relationship can only work if it's based on communication, and at the first difficult moment, you lie. That hurts."

"I'm so sorry," Cameron says, burying his head into Jay's shoulder. "If I could take it back, I would. I don't know how to make it right."

"Were cookies part of the plan?" I ask, eyeing the heart-shaped cookies laid out across his countertop.

My teasing finally gets Cameron to look at me, but he hasn't given up on punishing himself. He's all earnestness as he says, "They were just supposed to get me in the door. Mrs. Hill said I had to come bearing gifts if I wanted you to hear me out. We brainstormed what might mean something to you and decided for me to give a shot at something that means so much to you, Jay."

"And then?" I prompt.

"And then, I'd tell you that I'm done hiding. I'd introduce you to my family. I thought, maybe if you both gave me another chance, they could get to know you while you're still here. They want to know you. Celeste gave me almost as stern a talking-to as Mrs. Hill did. I can't promise I won't make a stupid mistake again, because I'm sure I will. But I'll do anything for another chance." Cameron's chest shudders with panicked breaths. "Please. Boone, before all this happened, I got to tell Jay how I feel, but I never got to tell you. I love you, Boone. I love you both. So much."

I rest a palm against Cameron's cheek, pulling Jay forward with my other hand until I can reach his face too.

"And I love you both," I say, my fingers reiterating the words with touch. "I'm always going to love you both."

Cameron closes his eyes and buries his head in his hands. Horrible sobs erupt and Jay and I both scurry to surround him with our arms and our bodies. I kiss his neck, while Jay caresses his temple. We soothe away his fear until the only thing left is love.

"I was so scared," Cameron says in between gasping breaths. His body still shakes from the release and the relief. "I don't know what I'd do without you."

"Don't you get it, sweetheart?" Jay says, his lips drawing trails along Cameron's ear and neck. "We aren't a we without you. You're the heart that binds us all together."

Jay leans forward and kisses Cameron until there's no more air. He pulls me forward with a directness that means my bossy Jay is back, and I don't even try to hide my joy. My smile hits Cameron's full lips as Jay directs our kiss.

"I think I'm supposed to be doing something with the cookies right now," Cameron says, his voice a little foggy when we part.

Jay sniffs the air.

"Nothing's on fire. We're good."

The three of us move back together, kissing and loving, knowing that our relationship has weathered its first trial. There will be more, but together, we can face anything.

EPILOGUE

6 MONTHS LATER

JAY

"Stop pacing, I'm sure he's fine."

I glance over my shoulder at Cameron, who calmly sits in the recliner, reading a book. His foot gives him away. It taps nervously on the floor. Taking that as permission, I return to my post at the front window, watching for Boone to return.

After finishing a semester of required classes, Boone is finally taking the exam for his teaching certificate. If all goes well, then he begins work as the assistant coach of Poudre Junior High after the holidays. Cameron and I helped him study all week, and I think we're more nervous about his test than he is.

"He should have been home by now," I whine. "What if he didn't pass and is out drowning his sorrows somewhere? What if he was in an accident and didn't even make it to the test?"

Two strong arms surround me with love and warmth. "He'll be home soon. Why don't you go bake more of those delicious Christmas cookies and we can celebrate when he gets home?"

Home. A modest house in the central part of town with only

two bedrooms, one that serves as our actual bedroom and another that functions as an office that we can all use. The kicker, and the reason Cam insisted this was the place for us, was the professional kitchen. The previous owner used to run a home cupcake catering business, and Cam said the space might give me ideas. I don't think I'm going to want to start anything on my own any time soon, but then again, he might have just hoped it would inspire me to bake for the two of them more often. It has certainly worked out that way.

In a week, Cam's whole family is going to be here to celebrate Christmas with us. Thankfully, they're staying at a hotel and not trying to cram in with us, but my kitchen is going to be stretched to the limit on Christmas Day. Boone's family did such a number on him that he's nervous as fuck to meet Cam's, so even though I'm nervous too, I try not to show it.

We went to my family's place for Thanksgiving, and I had to cage him and plug him and torture him for hours afterward, just to keep his mind from replaying every detail and worrying. And my family is pretty great. They were a little shocked at the three of us, but they tried not to let it show. My sister pulled me aside and congratulated me but warned me that I better not try any attention-stealing stunts next year, because she wanted all eyes on the baby and not thinking about threesome gay sex.

If anyone in my family is picturing me having sex, then that's their issue, not mine.

But I gave her the finally finished baby blanket, and she forgave me for stealing the limelight from her big ol' stomach and swollen feet. Cameron gave her a foot massage, which helped.

"He is so getting it for making me worry like this," I mutter and snuggle back into Cam's embrace. His lips caress the outer shell of my ear, making me shiver, and giving him an excuse to hold me even tighter.

"Remember, you promised me no punishments tonight. I want to reward Boone for all of his hard work."

"But my punishments are rewards."

"Don't you want to make me happy too, my beautiful bird?"

He continues to make me shiver until I give in.

"Fine. I promise. Tighter."

Cameron grips me impossibly tighter, his body blanketing mine as we watch out the window for Boone's new truck. He hated driving his old car from college, and we convinced him that a new truck with bench seats where we can all snuggle up together would be well worth the investment. He did *not* get it from Super Motors.

"Cookies?"

"No, I want to wait."

My eyes drift shut despite wanting to watch for Boone. This time last year, as I witnessed all the happy couples forming around me, I was convinced I would never find love of my own. I convinced myself I couldn't have it all – someone who wanted a toppy twink to both dominate them and love them. Now, I not only have that, but someone who wants to care for me too.

The happiness that fills me pours out around us, as Cameron insisted I fill our new home with love too. Everywhere you turn, I've placed some sort of reminder of the three of us and the bond we share. I even made Boone and Cam take part in some of the crafting – more collages but this time with pictures of us and our adventures over the past few months. And while the results were something you might expect from a kindergarten class, I'm as proud to display their contributions in our home as I am to display our relationship to the world. I love these two men and I'm no longer afraid who knows it.

Finally, a shiny black pickup ambles down the street at a slow pace, probably watching for kids that always play around the yards. The next-door-neighbor's kid loves to play Harry

Potter, and because of my hair, has decided that I'm Draco Malfoy. He calls our yard the Forbidden Forest, and he and his friends dare each other to infiltrate. I've been tempted to hide things in the bushes to scare them – plastic snakes or fake potions – just to see what they'd do.

Seeing Boone's truck makes me even more tense, as now I'm back to being worried about his test results. Cameron laughs against my hair and presses kisses onto the back of my neck.

"Calm down. Even if he didn't pass, we're going to be here for him and help him get there next time. Right?"

"Of course. I just don't want him to be disappointed. Not that I think he will be. He's super smart. I'm sure he did great."

"It's a relief to know you think I'm super smart." Boone's voice surprises us both. We'd been in such a daze watching him park, we hadn't even noticed him approaching the house. Or at least I hadn't. From the huffs of laughter against my hair, I think Cameron played me again.

"I'd hate to have to go into class next month and tell them how my boyfriend didn't think I was smart enough to become a teacher." Boone's mouth twists in a barely controlled grin.

I wriggle out of Cameron's arms and give Boone a light smack on his shoulder. "You shouldn't tease me, you know. I'll take it out on your hide later." Boone presses a kiss against my cheek, melting me enough to add, "Obviously I know you're smart enough to be a teacher. Who egged you on about it in the first place?"

"I can't believe you'd threaten to punish me, today of all days!" Boone crosses his arms and purses his lips into a pretty pout that I want to kiss away.

"I think all this time with Jay is teaching you how to be more of a brat, not less of one," Cameron says, wrapping his arms around Boone's waist and lifting him in the air. "Congratulations, sweetness. I'm so proud of you."

Boone laughs and begs to be put down, but then pouts again when Cameron complies.

"Oh, you're begging for a lesson, aren't you?" Boone's eyes light up and I gather Cameron in one arm and Boone in the other. "I promised Cam no punishments today, only rewards. By the time we're done with you, sweet thing, you're going to be begging us to stop rewarding you."

Cameron emits a sound of sheer delight, while Boone's eyes widen and he lets out a whimper.

"To the bedroom. Both of you."

CAMERON

I sit on the bed, eagerly anticipating what kind of rewards Jay has in mind. I've never had such a creative or bossy lover, and I love it, even when it's not directed at me. Watching my lithe, beautiful man know what he wants and go after it fills me with pride, knowing that I'm a part of what he wants.

"You two have fun while I get things ready," Jay tosses out over his shoulder as he heads to the dresser and his drawer of toys. Or torture, as Boone calls it.

Boone doesn't hesitate to approach, and he leans down, cradling my head in his hands and directing our kiss. His lips start soft and needy, begging mine to return his kiss, but I'm all out of patience. I may not have let Jay see it, but I was nervous for Boone too. Now that he's back, safe and sound and successful, I want to give him everything I have. I deepen the kiss, urging his mouth open with my tongue and tasting him. Our teeth clack inelegantly, but I don't care. My hands pull until his body is pressed against mine, his legs straddling me. His hands move lower, gripping at my neck until I'm sure there will be dots of fingertips at the back. His chest heaves into mine as I breathe everything, my worry and relief and pride, into him.

Fingertips dip under the collar of my shirt, desperate for more skin, but I don't want to let him go long enough to undress. When he whines in frustration, I give in and hold his bottom with one hand, using the other to jerk at my shirt buttons, eventually ripping them away in frustration and baring my chest.

"Jesus," Jay mutters from across the room, and I open my eyes to find him leaning against the dresser, shirt off, pants pushed down around his thighs, gripping his cock at the base as he watches us.

He approaches, laying some things on the bedside table, then sidles up behind Boone. I feel skin against mine as Jay lifts Boone's shirt. Boone gasps into my mouth, and I open my eyes again. Jay mouths at the back of Boone's neck, but it's the hand I feel between us, rubbing Boone's cock and grazing mine with the backs of knuckles, that causes the tortured sound to vibrate from Boone against my raw lips.

"I ... I ..." Boone's lips no longer clash with mine. His mind has drifted from me to the sensations from Jay. I lean back, my aching cock desperate for release from my jeans, and watch as Jay puts on a show for me.

His hands tweak Boone's nipples and slide across the lovely exposed skin when Boone gasps. One hand runs up and down the washboard abs on display while his other tangles into the small patch of hair in the middle of Boone's chest. Boone's head lolls back against Jay's shoulder as Jay continues to feast upon his neck with soft nibbles interspersed with playful bites. With my hands free, I help them out, unzipping Boone's jeans and opening them far enough to release his cock. When Jay's hand captures mine and we both give Boone a tight stroke, he shouts out a string of obscenities.

"We're going to have so much fun rewarding you, sweetness," I say, keeping my grip tight around his shaft with one hand, and working on my own zipper with the other. I really need to start wearing sweatpants around the house like Jay. Easier access.

Jay pulls Boone off me until Boone's feet are back on the floor. "First reward, suck Cam's cock. Scoot back, baby," Jay says to me, and I move until I'm fully on the bed.

"Remove your shirt," Jay tells me, and I comply as easily as Boone. He whispers something in Boone's ear, and soon, Boone has me stripped of my pants and briefs as well.

"Hands and knees."

Before I can think about the command enough to comprehend what Jay wants, Boone is on the bed between my legs, his knees pushing my legs farther apart and his hands bracing him on the bed on either side of my hips. A tongue digs at my foreskin, lapping around my sensitive head until I'm quickly hard enough for it to protrude on its own, deep purple and throbbing in time with my heartbeat.

Boone slowly works his tongue around, getting more of me wet and taking me further into his mouth with small thrusts to start. When he has about half my length wet and warm in his mouth, he lets out a shocked hum that vibrates around me, leaving me tingling at the sensation. I lift my head, hoping to see what caused his reaction, and find Jay kneeling behind Boone, his face buried into his ass.

I try to stifle my own moans, hoping to hear the soft, wet sounds of Jay's tongue opening Boone up, but Boone's own slurping around my cock is too noisy. He takes me all the way in, and I can no longer look, my head crashing back into the bedding and the ceiling sparkling with stars.

Jay's sweet breath sweeps across my face as he leans across the bed. "Do you want to watch and help as I prepare him? Or do you want him to keep sucking you?"

"Watch," I moan. Boone's mouth is heaven, but I love the

dirty sight of his hole opening up for us, and I have my first inkling of what Jay's reward is going to be.

For months now, we've been working on training Boone to take both of us. We've had a cock and fingers inside him, and even gone so far as a cock and a dildo inside, but we have yet to actually have both of our cocks in him at the same time. I've masturbated to the fantasy practically daily, and I have to focus to keep myself from popping off at the suggestion that the fantasy is about to come true.

Jay maneuvers Boone until he's in the middle of the bed, facing the headboard, still on his hands and knees. Boone's body racks with shivers, and Jay tells me to go comfort him for a bit. I kiss every inch of Boone's face, his eyelids and nose, down his throat, the tips of his ears. I stroke his neck and appreciate the strength in his shoulder with the swell of my lips. When his breathing finally returns to an anxious normal, I keep my hands on him, soothing him, but scoot down so that I can watch.

Jay starts small, with a dildo that he has coated with a generous amount of lube. Boone's hole easily accepts it, and we both groan, watching the dildo disappear before Jay begins to push and pull it in and out of Boone's body.

I reach underneath Boone to take his velvety shaft in my palm. I don't stroke – I know he'd go off at any moment if I did – but I hold it firmly, loving the weight and feel of it in my hand. My own cock hangs low and heavy, fully engorged now and ready to join the party. Maybe I need a cock cage of my own, because I don't see how I'm going to last.

Jay whispers sweet words as he adds his index finger, stretching Boone's hole until both the dildo and his finger thrust slowly inside.

"Give me your hand," Jay whispers to me and I let him lube up my finger. I have to change my position on the bed, but I shift so that we both have a hand around the dildo, each of us thrusting it and our slick fingers into Boone. He groans and drops his head onto his arms, his body shaking with the intrusion. A sheen of sweat covers his back and I use my free hand to wipe him down as Jay adds another finger, and then another of mine.

Boone's beautiful like this, shuddering and vulnerable and open. His hole is stretched and red and shiny with lube, and I need to be inside him. I've never felt this way about anyone before, but the way Boone trusts us with his body makes me want to join our bodies together so that he will always be ours.

Jay watches him with an expression that I think probably mirrors my own. He catches me, and smiles softly, leaning forward and pressing our lips together. It isn't hungry like my kiss with Boone earlier. It's the tender expression of two people sharing something magical and meaningful. It's love, so strong I can see it and feel it.

"I love you, beautiful bird," I whisper against his lips, our fingers touching inside Boone's passage, uniting us all together in a brief taste of what's to come.

My heart has never felt so full.

BOONE

It's so much. The stretch and the burn and the feeling of both of their hands inside me. Almost too much, but yet I want more. I want it all. My body shakes with desire and need, and maybe even a little bit of fear that they won't follow through and give me what I need, or if they do, I won't be able to handle it. My brain spins in a billion different directions to match the kaleidoscope of sensations racking my body.

It's so much, and then it's nothing.

"Shh," Cameron whispers against my shoulder when I hadn't realized I was crying out. "I've got you."

He lies underneath me and pulls my body over his. Sweat slicks between us, but his skin feels cool, or maybe it's just that I'm burning up with want. Our cocks slide together, and he wraps his arms around me until I'm trapped and secure.

"Oh," I say on a sigh, my body relaxing at the knowledge that Cameron has me.

I let myself drift on a cloud of comfort until something wet drizzles down my crack, shocking me back to reality.

"You've been so good for us already," Jay's voice comes from somewhere. "It's time for your reward."

Cameron's arms stay around me, so I know it must be Jay who guides Cameron's cock against my hole. It slips and slides and then the tip catches on my rim and I bite back a groan as Jay presses it forward.

"Yes," Jay says. "Open for Cam, baby. That's it. So lovely. I wish you could see what it looks like, your hole opening around his cock. Such an eager hole for our eager slut."

I think I'm going to burst into flames, I'm so hot from Jay's teasing.

"I thought no punishments?" Cameron's voice vibrates against my shoulder and I jolt at the words.

"Calling our Boone a slut isn't a punishment. It's praise. He's our beautiful slut, ready to take both of our cocks. Aren't you, Boone?"

I'm not sure what sound comes out of my mouth, but it makes Cameron catch his breath and Jay groan and congratulate himself on being right. I'm their slut and it's lovely and good. I'm lovely and good, and I'm going to take them both.

Something else nudges against my hole. Jay's hand soothes up and down my sweat-slicked back, and he whispers kind, sweet words to relax me. I follow his instructions, taking a deep breath and holding it, clenching my hole as tight as I can around Cameron's cock, then releasing with an exaggerated sigh as Jay stretches my hole with his cock sliding against Cameron's.

"Yesss," Jay hisses and Cameron moans. My head spins and falls against the pillow over Cameron's shoulder. I can't move, can't think, can't do anything but lie here and take it and feel.

And I feel so much.

With each tiny shift, it feels like every single nerve ending in my body has congregated in my ass for this event, to torment me with too much feeling. I shudder and shake and Cameron does his best to hold me as Jay continues to fill me, inch by mind-blowing inch.

Soon, I hear him say, "I'm in," and the last of my tension bleeds from my body, leaving me a rag doll. A happy rag doll who's about to explode in every direction from the fireworks going off in every pore of his body.

My cock is trapped between my body and Cameron's, and my dick gives a valiant attempt at seeking friction as it jumps from a jolt of blood rushing into it. Now that the hard part is over, my cock is remembering why he thought this was such a good idea, but there's no way to reach a hand between us. Hopefully Jay meant what he said, and I'm going to be allowed to come.

Jay starts to move, a shallow thrust as his breaths beat against my overheated back.

"Oh God," Cameron says with a moan, "I'm not going to last."

"You are," Jay says with the demanding voice he usually reserves for me. "Because you want to make this special for Boone. Boone gets to come first, and then we're going to fill him with our cum and plug him up and make him hold it inside all night long."

Fucking hell. If Jay keeps talking like that, I don't think I'll even need Cameron's hand on me to come. We all got tested last month and have started to go without condoms. The thought of their seed inside me, marking me, was too hot. But even more, it was the fact that they both trusted me, even though they knew I had cheated before. I think that decision meant more to me than our deciding to buy a house together. It was truly the symbol of our lasting commitment.

"Yes, please," I moan into the pillow and Cam's neck. "Make me yours."

"Then you know what you need to do, sweetheart. You need to come."

The pressure against my prostate has nothing on the effect that command has coming from Jay's thin and talented lips. I shout both of their names as I feel the pressure build until it's too much to hold. My cum shoots between our bodies, making us even more slippery. Hands grab at my body everywhere as the blood pumps harder and harder around my head with each heavy pulse of my release.

When it's finally finished, Jay starts to move with long, hard strokes that have Cameron shouting at each one.

"Yes, fuck, yes!"

"That's it, Cam. Fill him up. Come on my dick, deep inside our Boone."

My hole gets even more slippery as Cameron's warm cum fills my hole and dribbles out with each of Jay's continuing thrusts.

"I'm coming too," Jay says with a groan, his voice finally punctuated with the effort of his release. "Fuck. Love you both."

I feel Jay shift on top of me as a hand bats around somewhere to my right. I crack open an eye to see him grabbing at a plug he had waiting on the nightstand. I'm too sated to do anything but lie still and let Jay take charge, pulling out of my body and inserting the waiting plug around the dripping mess of my hole.

Fingers run through the cum that has already been fucked free, and I shiver.

"Tickles," I mumble and hear Jay laugh.

"Good. Don't want you to get too used to all this reward and no punishment."

"Can you move?" Cameron asks from underneath me. I stopped trying to keep myself from squishing him long ago, so he's probably ready for me to get off.

"I think so."

My legs wobble and I catch myself on the bed before Jay rushes over to throw my arm around his shoulder. Cameron gets the other side and they walk me to the shower.

"Need new sheets," I say, my overstimulated brain catching on weird things, like the sweat- and cum-soaked sheets in the corner of my eye, or the way Jay is the perfect height to tuck under my arm.

"Let's get cleaned up first, sweetness. Then let us worry about the sheets. You just rest."

Jay props me against the wall while he and Cameron take turns washing themselves and washing me. Their gentle hands clean sore and stretched places, and Cameron bends down to bestow a sweet kiss against my swollen pucker.

When Jay brings me back to bed, fresh sheets have magically appeared and Jay and Cameron position me in the middle of the bed. I know that come morning, I'll have one of Cameron's limbs draped across me and Jay's face snuggled into my chest. Exactly the way I like it.

For now, we spoon together like a set of Russian dolls, biggest to smallest, with me happily sandwiched in the middle.

I'm marked and sated and loved in ways I never thought possible, in a relationship I never dreamed I would be brave enough to try. But I'll try anything for these two men. Only for them.

ACKNOWLEDGMENTS

I always have so many wonderful friends to thank every time I put out a new book. First and foremost, I'd like to thank my fellow authors and readers for all the words of encouragement along the way. I love writing, and as a world-class introvert, I often think I'd be just has happy to continue writing only for myself and never publish another word. It's your excitement over a new series or next book that makes venturing into public (the horror!) worthwhile.

Thank you to Leslie Copeland and Courtney Bassett for making this book better. Your hard work makes mine look effortless, and I love you both! Thank you to DJ Jamison for your valuable input and for being the best mirror twin a girl could want! And finally, Garrett Leigh, for the gorgeous cover. Truly, I could look at it all day. And night. Sigh.

ALSO BY JD CHAMBERS

Only Colorado Series:

Only with You - Zach and Craig
Only See You - Mal and Parker
Only Need You - Kieran and Ted
Only Keep You - Dave and Arthur
Only Love You - Ben and Jonathan
Only for Us - Cameron, Jay, and Boone

Natural Hearts Series:

Depth of Focus - Travis and Whitman

Reject Romance Series:

Trolling for Love - A Reject Romance Short Story

Short Story Series:

The Incredibly Raw Adventures of Sven and Victor
Paper Cup Beginnings
Lakeside Interludes
Haunted Hijinx

ABOUT THE AUTHOR

JD Chambers wanted at various times to be Indiana Jones, Pat Benatar, and Wonder Woman when she grew up. She never considered writing down the stories she crafted in her head. They provided nothing more than entertainment for long drives or sleepless nights, until one particular story insisted it didn't want to reside only in her noggin. She hasn't stopped writing since.

JD finds unlikely heroes, humans courageous enough to be themselves, and spreadsheets incredibly sexy -- the last one much to her husband's chagrin. Together, they raise three teenagers and the world's most mellow Chihuahua on the Oregon Coast.

For updates and information,
subscribe to JD's newsletter at
www.subscribepage.com/jdsnewsletter

Made in the USA
Coppell, TX
10 October 2023

22666745R00142